Quest of the Three Worlds

An immortal turtle-girl...the wind people of Henriada...a mad go-captain...a race of beings gabbling their hatred of humanity to the listening stars...a city devoted to absolute perfection ...the Deep Dry Lake of the Damned Irene...

Casher O'Neill encountered them all on his self-imposed mission—until his final meeting with a Lady of the Instrumentality and a prophet's vision that their bones would whiten together in the desert wind...

Eerie, touching, dramatic—and with a vein of wry humor—*Quest of the Three Worlds* is a richly colorful panel of the great tapestry of the future that Cordwainer Smith crafted in the body of work that has won him a unique place in the literature of the imagination.

Quest of the Three Worlds

Cordwainer Smith

A Del Rey Book

BALLANTINE BOOKS • NEW YORK

Introduction

Meet Casher O'Neill: adventurer, pilgrim, mystic and—a street in downtown Cairo?

Paul Myron Anthony Linebarger (1913–1966) who (you must know by now) was secretly Cordwainer Smith until shortly before his death, delighted in decorating his stories with cryptic puns, references, and allusions—so many that they haven't all been sorted out even yet.

Qasr El Nil is a street in downtown Cairo. And if you know that the people who live there call their country *Misr*, not Egypt, you won't have any trouble interpreting Mizzer. Kuraf, Wedder and Gibna are, of course, anagrams on the names of the Egyptian king and the two colonels who overthrew him. And why, given all this, was Qasr El Nil transformed into Casher O'Neill? Smith wanted to convey the idea of an adventurer, and an Irish name seemed to fit.

Readers can be forgiven if they fail to realize why Casher finds it so appropriate for the planet Pontoppidan to have a capital named Andersen (Henrik Pontoppidan was a Danish author, and Andersen a hero of his *Soil*—a commodity lacking on the gem planet). Or that the stormy world of Henriada was largely inspired by Smith's memory of a childhood experience with a hurricane in Biloxi, Mississippi. Or that he expressed his concern with the violence of the 1960s by creating passages in which the first letters of each sentence spell out "KENNEDY SHOT" and "OSWALD SHOT TOO."*

*See pp. 78 and 83–84.

Such esoterica, fortunately, are not essential to the enjoyment of *Quest of the Three Worlds*. For the story of Casher O'Neill, like nearly all of Smith's science fiction, is part of the vast epic of the Instrumentality of Mankind that has been fascinating readers for more than twenty years.

Most of that epic has already been collected in *Norstrilia* and *The Best of Cordwainer Smith*, and the present volume; the remaining stories completed by Paul Linebarger during his lifetime will be included in a fourth volume, appropriately titled *The Instrumentality of Mankind*. There may be more to come: Linebarger's widow Genevieve, who collaborated with him on several stories, has written others based on uncompleted manuscripts or ideas they had discussed—and Linebarger left tape-recorded notes for still other stories.

Be that as it may, the Casher O'Neill stories come at the end of the cycle of tales and legends that had been completed at the time of Linebarger's death. It is the second century of the Rediscovery of Man, a vast undertaking by the Lords of the Instrumentality and their covert allies among the underpeople to undo (at least partly) the suffocating utopia to which the Lords themselves had subjected mankind for millennia.

Since the Instrumentality, at this time, is in the business of recreating cultures of the Ancient World as part of its program to restore freedom and diversity to human existence, Cordwainer Smith had a perfect science-fictional justification for Mizzer—Kuraf, Wedder, Gibna, and all. But he could also create worlds like none ever seen: Pontoppidan, where gems are worthless and earth is precious; Henriada, with its air whales and wind people. Smith's worlds are bizarre, but they *work*.

As always, there are allusions to figures and incidents from ages past: Go-Captain Magno Taliano, legendary hero of "The Burning of the Brain," and the Kaskaskia Effect, a mind-destroying weapon of Earth's Dark Age. There are allusions, too, to stories that were yet to be written when Paul Linebarger died: one of these concerned The Robot, the Rat and the Copt, whose visions are referred to herein.

But at the center of *Quest of the Three Worlds* is the personality of Casher O'Neill himself. Although part four (originally "Three to a Given Star"), with its self-parody of Smith's animal-derived cultures, is tangential to the others, the theme of most of the book is Casher's spiritual quest rather than travel or adventure as such.

Paul Linebarger, as has been said elsewhere, was deeply religious, and in most of his science fiction he seemed to be trying to reconcile the visions of Christianity and science, of evolution and Revelation. Whether he had fully developed his ideas on the destiny of mankind, we may never know. For *Quest of the Three Worlds,* it doesn't matter: it is a story of personal salvation rather than human destiny.

One could compare the work rather loosely to *Pilgrim's Progress.* The Lords of the Instrumentality, as materialist utopians, had sought for thousands of years to eradicate the spiritual, and even in Casher's time they maintain an embargo on the spread of religion. The underpeople, some of whom have obviously symbolic names like D'Alma (*Alma* = "soul" in Spanish) and T'Ruth, are almost the only custodians of the Old Strong Religion, and are thus appropriate guides for his pilgrimage.

It isn't all merely a matter of symbology, of course. Until the Rediscovery of Man, few men have faced the agony of moral consciousness and moral choice: all decisions have been made for them by the Instrumentality. Casher O'Neill, like others of his time, must rediscover what it means to be a free human being; if he also discovers the secrets of Christianity, it is only as a free man that they can have any meaning for him.

No doubt one could find some parallels to Bunyan in grotesque characters such as Murray Madigan and John Joy Tree, as well as in the role of the underpeople spiritual guides. And Casher is very much like Bunyan's pilgrim in his progress past the temptations of the City of Hopeless Hope, Kermesse Dorgueil, and the Deep Dry Lake of the Damned Irene. But we should not try to stretch parallels too far; the Thirteenth Nile is not necessarily Heaven, and can be understood better allegorically, as a state of the soul.

In any case, don't be put off by such parallels. *Pilgrim's Progress* once turned up on a list of "classics" that had bored the most readers, but Cordwainer Smith is never boring. Like the rest of his works, *Quest of the Three Worlds* is filled with invention, from the funny robot who doesn't know what to make of the "improper" object coming out of the Hippy Dipsy to the dramatic journey across Henriada in a tank that anchors itself to the ground to avoid being blown away.

If you've read anything else by Smith, you don't need this introduction to tell you how good he can be. But if *Quest of the Three Worlds* is your first exposure to this unique mythographer of a bizarre and wonderful imaginary future, you won't want to miss any of the rest. Smith's universe, sooner or later, must be experienced as a whole.

John J. Pierce
Berkeley Heights, N.J.
June 7, 1978

Part One

Consider the horse. He climbed up through the crevasses of a cliff of gems; the force which drove him was the love of man.

Consider Mizzer, the resort planet, where the dictator Colonel Wedder reformed the culture so violently that whatever had been slovenly now became atrocious.

Consider Genevieve, so rich that she was the prisoner of her own wealth, so beautiful that she was the victim of her own beauty, so intelligent that she knew there was nothing, nothing to be done about her fate.

Consider Casher O'Neill, a wanderer among the planets, thirsting for justice and yet hoping in his innermost thoughts that "justice" was not just another word for revenge.

Consider Pontoppidan, that literal gem of a planet, where the people where too rich and busy to have good food, open air or much fun. All they had were diamonds, rubies, tourmalines and emeralds.

Add these together and you have one of the strangest stories ever told from world to world.

I

When Casher O'Neill came to Pontoppidan, he found that the capital city was appropriately called Andersen.

This was the second century of the Rediscovery of Man. People everywhere had taken up old names, old languages, old customs, as fast as the robots and the underpeople could retrieve the data from the rubbish of forgotten starlanes or the subsurface ruins of Manhome itself.

Casher knew this very well, to his bitter cost. Reacculturation had brought him revolution and exile. He came from the dry, beautiful planet of Mizzer. He was himself the nephew of the ruined ex-ruler, Kuraf, whose collection of objectionable books had at one time been unmatched in the settled galaxy; he had stood aside, half-assenting, when the colonels Gibna and Wedder took over the planet in the name of reform; he had implored the Instrumentality, vainly, for help when Wedder became a tyrant; and now he traveled among the stars, looking for men or weapons who might destroy Wedder and make Kaheer again the luxurious, happy city which it once had been.

He felt that his cause was hopeless when he landed on Pontoppidan. The people were warm-hearted, friendly, intelligent, but they had no motives to fight for, no weapons to fight with, no enemies to fight against. They had little public spirit, such as Casher O'Neill had seen back on his native planet of Mizzer. They were concerned about little things.

Indeed, at the time of his arrival, the Pontoppidans were wildly excited about a horse.

A horse! Who worries about one horse?

Casher O'Neill himself said so. "Why bother about a horse? We have lots of them on Mizzer. They are four-handed beings, eight times the weight of a man, with only one finger on each of the four hands. The fingernail is very heavy and permits them to run fast. That's why our people have them, for running."

"Why run?" said the Hereditary Dictator of Pontoppidan. "Why run, when you can fly? Don't you have orni-thopters?"

"We don't run with them," said Casher indignantly. "We make them run against each other and then we pay prizes to the one which runs fastest."

"But then," said Philip Vincent, the Hereditary Dictator, "you get a very illogical situation. When you have tried out these four-fingered beings, you know how fast each one goes. So what? Why bother?"

His niece interrupted. She was a fragile little thing, smaller than Casher O'Neill liked women to be. She had clear gray eyes, well-marked eyebrows, a very artificial coiffure of silver-blonde hair and the most sensitive little mouth he had ever seen. She conformed to the local fashion by wearing some kind of powder or face cream which was flesh-pink in color but which had overtones of lilac. On a woman as old as twenty-two, such a coloration would have made the wearer look like an old hag, but on Genevieve it was pleasant, if rather startling. It gave the effect of a happy child playing grown-up and doing the job joyfully and well. Casher knew that it was hard to tell ages in those off-trail planets. Genevieve might be a grand dame in her third or fourth rejuvenation.

He doubted it, on second glance. What she said was sensible, young, and pert:

"But uncle, they're *animals!*"

"I know that," he rumbled.

"But uncle, don't you see it?"

"Stop saying 'but uncle' and tell me what you mean," growled the Dictator, very fondly.

"Animals are always *uncertain*."

"Of course," said the uncle.

"That makes it a game, uncle," said Genevieve. "They're never sure that any one of them would do the same thing twice. Imagine the excitement—the beautiful big beings from earth running around and around on their four middle fingers, the big fingernails making the gems jump loose from the ground!"

"I'm not at all sure it's that way. Besides, Mizzer may be covered with something valuable, such as earth or sand, instead of gemstones like the ones we have here on Pontoppidan. You know your flower-pots with their rich, warm, wet, soft earth?"

"Of course I do, uncle. And I know what you paid for them. You were very generous. And still are," she added diplomatically, glancing quickly at Casher O'Neill to see how the familial piety went across with the visitor.

"We're not that rich on Mizzer. It's mostly sand, with farmland along the Twelve Niles, our big rivers."

"I've seen pictures of rivers," said Genevieve. "Imagine living on a whole world full of flowerpot stuff!"

"You're getting off the subject, darling. We were wondering why anyone would bring one horse, just one horse, to Pontoppidan. I suppose you could race a horse against himself, if you had a stopwatch. But would it be fun? Would you do that, young man?"

Casher O'Neill tried to be respectful. "In my home I used to have a lot of horses. I've seen my uncle time them one by one."

"Your uncle?" said the Dictator interestedly. "Who was your uncle that he had all these four-fingered 'horses' running around? They're all Earth animals and very expensive."

Casher felt the coming of the low, slow blow he had met so many times before, right from the whole outside world into the pit of his stomach. "My uncle"—he stammered—"my uncle—I thought you knew—was the old Dictator of Mizzer, Kuraf."

Philip Vincent jumped to his feet, very lightly for so well-fleshed a man. The young mistress, Genevieve, clutched at the throat of her dress.

"Kuraf!" cried the old Dictator. "Kuraf! We know about him, even here. But you were supposed to be a Mizzer patriot, not one of Kuraf's people."

"He doesn't have any children—" Casher began to explain.

"I should think not, not with those habits!" snapped the old man.

"—so I'm his nephew and his heir. But I'm not trying to put the Dictatorship back, even though I should be dictator. I just want to get rid of Colonel Wedder. He has ruined my people, and I am looking for money or weapons to help to make my home-world free." This was the point, Casher O'Neill knew, at which people either started believing him or did not. If they did not, there was not much he could do about it. If they did, he was sure to get some sympathy. So far, no help. Just sympathy.

But the Instrumentality, while refusing to take action against Colonel Wedder, had given young Casher O'Neill an all-world travel pass—something which a hundred lifetimes of savings could not have purchased for the ordinary man. (His obscene old uncle had gone off to Sunvale, on Ttiollé, the resort planet, to live out his years between the casino and the beach.) Casher O'Neill held the conscience of Mizzer in his hand. Only he, among the star travelers, cared enough to fight for the freedom of the

Twelve Niles. Here, now, in this room, there was a turning point.

"I won't give you anything," said the Hereditary Dictator, but he said it in a friendly voice. His niece started tugging at his sleeve.

The older man went on. "Stop it, girl. I won't give you anything, not if you're part of that rotten lot of Kuraf's, not unless—"

"Anything, sir, anything, just so that I get help or weapons to go home to the Twelve Niles!"

"All right, then. Unless you open your mind to me. I'm a good telepath myself."

"Open my mind! Whatever for?" The incongruous indecency of it shocked Casher O'Neill. He'd had men and women and governments ask a lot of strange things from him, but no one before had had the cold impudence to ask him to open his mind. "And why you?" he went on, "What would you get out of it? There's nothing much in my mind."

"To make sure," said the Hereditary Dictator, "that you are not too honest and sharp in your beliefs. If you're positive that you know what to do, you might be another Colonel Wedder, putting your people through a dozen torments for a Utopia which never quite comes true. If you don't care at all, you might be like your uncle. He did no real harm. He just stole his planet blind and he had some extraordinary habits which got him talked about between the stars. He never killed a man in his life, did he?"

"No, sir," said Casher O'Neill, "he never did." It relieved him to tell the one little good thing about his uncle; there was so very, very little which could be said in Kuraf's favor.

"I don't like slobbering old libertines like your uncle," said Philip Vincent, "but I don't hate them either. They don't hurt other people much. As a matter of actual fact, they don't hurt anyone but themselves. They waste property, though. Like these horses you have on Mizzer. We'd never bring living beings to this world of Pontoppidan, just to play games with. And you know we're not poor. We're no Old North Australia, but we have a good income here."

That, thought Casher O'Neill, is the understatement of the year, but he was a careful young man with a great deal at stake, so he said nothing.

The Dictator looked at him shrewdly. He appreciated the value of Casher's tactful silence. Genevieve tugged at his sleeves, but he frowned her interruption away.

"If," said the Hereditary Dictator, "*if*," he repeated, "you pass two tests, I will give you a green ruby as big as my head. If my Committee will allow me to do so. But I think I can talk them around. One test is that you let me peep all over your mind, to make sure that I am not dealing with one more honest fool. If you're too honest, you're a fool and a danger to mankind. I'll give you a dinner and ship you off-planet as fast as I can. And the other test is— solve the puzzle of this horse. The one horse on Pontoppidan. Why is the animal here? What should we do with it? If it's good to eat, how should we cook it? Or can we trade to some other world, like your planet Mizzer, which seems to set a value on horses?"

"Thank you, sir—" said Casher O'Neill.

"But, uncle—" said Genevieve.

"Keep quiet, my darling, and let the young man speak," said the Dictator.

"—all I was going to ask, is," said Casher O'Neill, "what's a green ruby good for? I didn't even know they came green."

"That, young man, is a Pontoppidan specialty. We have a geology based on ultra-heavy chemistry. This planet was once a fragment from a giant planet which imploded. The use is simple. With a green ruby you can make a laser beam which will boil away your city of Kaheer in a single sweep. We don't have weapons here and we don't believe in them, so I won't give you a weapon. You'll have to travel further to find a ship and to get the apparatus for mounting your green ruby. *If* I give it to you. But you will be one more step along in your fight with Colonel Wedder."

"Thank you, thank you, most honorable sir!" cried Casher O'Neill.

"But uncle," said Genevieve, "you shouldn't have picked those two things because I know the answers."

"You know all about *him*," said the Hereditary Dictator, "by some means of your own?"

Genevieve flushed under her lilac-hued foundation cream. "I know enough for us to know."

"How do you know it, my darling?"

"I just know," said Genevieve.

Her uncle made no comment, but he smiled widely and indulgently as if he had heard that particular phrase before.

She stamped her foot. "And I know about the horse, too. *All* about it."

"Have you seen it?"

"No."

"Have you talked to it?"

"Horses don't talk, uncle."

"Most underpeople do," he said.

"This isn't an underperson, uncle. It's a plain unmodified old Earth animal. It never did talk."

"Then what do you know, my honey?" The uncle was affectionate, but there was the crackle of impatience under his voice.

"I taped it. The whole thing. The story of the horse of Pontoppidan. And I've edited it, too. I was going to show it to you this morning, but your staff sent that young man in."

Casher O'Neill looked his apologies at Genevieve.

She did not notice him. Her eyes were on her uncle.

"Since you've done this much, we might as well see it."
He turned to the attendants. "Bring chairs. And drinks. You

know mine. The young lady will take tea with lemon. Real tea. Will you have coffee, young man?"

"You have coffee!" cried Casher O'Neill. As soon as he said it, he felt like a fool. Pontoppidan was a *rich* planet. On most worlds' exchanges, coffee came out to about two man-years per kilo. Here halftracks crunched their way through gems as they went to load up the frequent trading vessels.

The chairs were put in place. The drinks arrived. The Hereditary Dictator had been momentarily lost in a brown study, as though he were wondering about his promise to Casher O'Neill. He had even murmured to the young man, "Our bargain stands? Never mind what my niece says." Casher had nodded vigorously. The old man had gone back to frowning at the servants and did not relax until a tiger-man bounded into the room, carrying a tray with acrobatic precision. The chairs were already in place.

The uncle held his niece's chair for her as a command that she sit down. He nodded Casher O'Neill into a chair on the other side of himself.

He commanded, "Dim the lights . . ."

The room plunged into semi-darkness.

Without being told, the people took their places immediately behind the three main seats and the underpeople perched or sat on benches and tables behind them. Very little was spoken. Casher O'Neill could sense that Pontoppidan was a well-run place. He began to wonder if the Hereditary Dictator had much real work left to do, if he could fuss that much over a single horse. Perhaps all he did was boss his niece and watch the robots load truckloads of gems into sacks while the underpeople weighed them, listed them and wrote out the bills for the customers.

II

There was no screen; this was a good machine.

The planet Pontoppidan came into view, its airless brightness giving strong hints of the mineral riches which might be found.

Here and there enormous domes, such as the one in which this palace was located, came into view.

Genevieve's own voice, girlish, impulsive and yet didactic, rang out with the story of her planet. It was as though she had prepared the picture not only for her own uncle but for off-world visitors as well. *By Joan, that's it!* thought Casher O'Neill. *If they don't raise much food here, outside of the hydroponics, and don't have any real People Places, they have to trade: that does mean visitors and many, many of them.*

The story was interesting, but the girl herself was more interesting. Her face shone in the shifting light which the images—a meter, perhaps a little more, from the floor—reflected across the room. Casher O'Neill thought that he had never before seen a woman who so peculiarly combined intelligence and charm. She was girl, girl, girl, all the way through; but she was also very smart and pleased with being smart. It betokened a happy life. He found himself glancing covertly at her. Once he caught her glancing, equally covertly at him. The darkness of the scene enabled them both to pass it off as an accident without embarrassment.

Her viewtape had come to the story of the *dipsies*,

enormous canyons which lay like deep gashes on the surface of the planet. Some of the color views were spectacular beyond belief. Casher O'Neill, as the "appointed one" of Mizzer, had had plenty of time to wander through the nonsalacious parts of his uncle's collections, and he had seen pictures of the most notable worlds.

Never had he seen anything like this. One view showed a sunset against a six-kilometer cliff of a material which looked like solid emerald. The peculiar bright sunshine of Pontoppidan's small, penetrating, lilac-hued sun ran like living water over the precipice of gems. Even the reduced image, one meter by one meter, was enough to make him catch his breath.

The bottom of the dipsy had vapor emerging in curious cylindrical columns which seemed to erode as they reached two or three times the height of a man. The recorded voice of Genevieve was explaining that the very thin atmosphere of Pontoppidan would not be breathable for another 2,520 years, since the settlers did not wish to squander their resources on a luxury like breathing when the whole planet only had 60,000 inhabitants; they would rather go on with masks and use their wealth in other ways. After all, it was not as though they did not have their domed cities, some of them many kilometers in radius. Besides the usual hydroponics, they had even imported 7.2 hectares of garden soil, 5.5 centimeters deep, together with enough water to make the gardens rich and fruitful. They had bought worms, too, at the price of eight carats of diamond per living worm, in order to keep the soil of the gardens loose and living.

Genevieve's transcribed voice rang out with pride as she listed these accomplishments of her people, but a note of sadness came in when she returned to the subject of the dipsies. ". . . and though we would like to live in them and develop their atmospheres, we dare not. There is too much escape of radioactivity. The geysers themselves may or may not be contaminated from one hour to the next. So we just look at them. Not one of them has ever been settled, except for the Hippy Dipsy, where the horse came from. Watch this next picture."

The camera sheered up, up, up from the surface of the planet. Where it had wandered among mountains of diamonds and valleys of tourmalines, it now took to the blueback of near, inner space. One of the canyons showed (from high altitude) the grotesque pattern of a human woman's hips and legs, though what might have been the upper body was lost in a confusion of broken hills which ended in a bright almost-iridescent plain to the North.

"That," said the real Genevieve, overriding her own voice on the screen, "is the Hippy Dipsy. There, see the blue? That's the only lake on all of Pontoppidan. And here we drop to the hermit's house."

Casher O'Neill almost felt vertigo as the camera plummeted from off-planet into the depths of that immense canyon. The edges of the canyon almost seemed to move like lips with the plunge, opening and folding inward to swallow him up.

Suddenly they were beside a beautiful little lake.

A small hut stood beside the shore.

In the doorway there sat a man, dead.

His body had been there a long time; it was already mummified.

Genevieve's recorded voice explained the matter: ". . . in Norstrilian law and custom, they told him that his time had come. They told him to go to the Dying House, since he was no longer fit to live. In Old North Australia, they are so rich that they let everyone live as long as he wants, unless the old person can't take rejuvenation any more, even with stroon, and unless he or she gets to be a real pest to the living. If that happens, they are invited to go to the Dying House, where they shriek and pant with delirious joy for weeks or days until they finally die of an overload of sheer happiness and excitement. . . ." There was a hesitation, even in the recording. "We never knew why this man refused. He stood off-planet and said that he had seen views of the Hippy Dipsy. He said it was the most beautiful place on all the worlds, and that he wanted to build a cabin there, to live alone, except for his non-human friend. We thought it was some small pet. When we told him that the Hippy Dipsy was very dangerous, he said that this did not matter in the least to him, since he was old and dying anyhow. Then he offered to pay us twelve times our planetary income if we would lease him twelve hectares on the condition of absolute privacy. No pictures, no scanners, no help, no visitors. Just solitude and scenery. His name was Perinö. My great-grandfather asked for nothing more, except the written transfer of credit. When he paid it, Perinö even asked that he be left alone after he was dead. Not even a vault rocket so that he could either orbit Pontoppidan forever or start a very slow journey to nowhere, the way so many people like it. So this is our first picture of him. We took it when the light went off in the People Room and one of the tigermen told us that he was sure a human consciousness had come to an end in the Hippy Dipsy.

"And we never even thought of the pet. After all, we had never made a picture of him. This is the way he arrived from Perinö's shack."

A robot was shown in a control room, calling excitedly in the old Common Tongue.

"People, people! Judgment needed! Moving object coming out of the Hippy Dipsy. Object has improper shape. Not a correct object. Should not rise. Does so anyhow. People, tell me, people, tell me! Destroy or not destroy? This is an improper object. It should fall, not rise. Coming out of the Hippy Dipsy."

A firm click shut off the robot's chatter. A well-shaped woman took over. From the nature of her work and the lithe, smooth tread with which she walked, Casher O'Neill suspected that she was of cat origin, but there was nothing in her dress or in her manner to show that she was under-people.

The woman in the picture lighted a screen.

She moved her hands in the air in front of her, like a blind person feeling his way through open day.

The picture on the inner screen came to resolution.

A face showed in it.

What a face! thought Casher O'Neill, and he heard the other people around him in the viewing room.

The horse!

Imagine a face like that of a newborn cat, thought Casher. Mizzer is full of cats. But imagine the face with a huge mouth, with big yellow teeth—a nose long beyond imagination. Imagine eyes which look friendly. In the picture they were rolling back and forth with exertion but even there—when they did not feel observed—there was nothing hostile about the set of the eyes. They were tame, companionable eyes. Two ridiculous ears stood high, and a little tuft of golden hair showed on the crest of the head between the ears.

The viewed scene was comical, too. The cat-woman was as astonished as the viewers. It was lucky that she had touched the emergency switch, so that she not only saw the horse, but had recorded herself and her own actions while bringing him into view.

Genevieve whispered across the chest of the Hereditary Dictator: "Later we found he was a palomino pony. That's a very special kind of horse. And Perinö had made him immortal, or almost immortal."

"Sh-h!" said her uncle.

The screen-within-the-screen showed the cat-woman waving her hands in the air some more. The view broadened.

The horse had four hands and no legs, or four legs and no hands, whichever way you want to count them.

The horse was fighting his way up a narrow cleft of rubies

which led out of the Hippy Dipsy. He panted heavily. The
oxygen bottles on his sides swung wildly as he clambered.
He must have seen something, perhaps the image of the cat-
woman, because he said a word:

Whay-yay-yay-yay-whay-yay!

The cat-woman in the nearer picture spoke very dis-
tinctly:

"Give your name, age, species and authority for being on
this planet." She spoke clearly and with the utmost possible
authority.

The horse obviously heard her. His ears tipped forward.
But his reply was the same as before:

Whay-yay-yay!

Casher O'Neill realized that he had followed the mood of
the picture and had seen the horse the way that the people on
Pontoppidan would have seen him. On second thought, the
horse was nothing special, by the standards of the Twelve
Niles or the Little Horse Market in the city of Kaheer. It was
an old pony stallion, no longer fit for breeding and probably
not for riding either. The hair had whitened among the gold;
the teeth were worn. The animal showed many injuries and
burns. Its only use was to be killed, cut up and fed to the
racing dogs. But he said nothing to the people around him.
They were still spellbound by the picture.

The cat-woman repeated:

"Your name isn't Whayayay. Identify yourself properly;
name first."

The horse answered her with the same word in a higher
key.

Apparently forgetting that she had recorded herself as
well as the emergency screen, the cat-woman said, "I'll call
real people if you don't answer! They'll be annoyed at being
bothered."

The horse rolled his eyes at her and said nothing.

The cat-woman pressed an emergency button on the side
of the room. One could not see the other communication

screen which lighted up, but her end of the conversation was plain.

"I want an ornithopter. Big one. Emergency."

A mumble from the side screen.

"To go to the Hippy Dipsy. There's an underperson there, and he's in so much trouble that he won't talk." From the screen beside her, the horse seemed to have understood the sense of the message, if not the words, because he repeated:

Whay-yay-whay-yay-yay!

"See," said the cat-woman to the person in the other screen, "that's what he's doing. It's obviously an emergency."

The voice from the other screen came through, tinny and remote by double recording:

"Fool, yourself, cat-woman! Nobody can fly an ornithopter into a dipsy. Tell your silly friend to go back to the floor of the dipsy and we'll pick him up by space rocket."

Whay-yay-yay! said the horse impatiently.

"He's not my *friend*," said the cat-woman with brisk annoyance. "I just discovered him a couple of minutes ago. He's asking for help. Any idiot can see that, even if we don't know his language."

The picture snapped off.

The next scene showed tiny human figures working with searchlights at the top of an immeasurably high cliff. Here and there, the beam of the searchlight caught the cliff face; the translucent faceted material of the cliff looked almost like rows of eerie windows, their lights snapping on and off, as the searchlight moved.

Far down there was a red glow. Fire came from inside the mountain.

Even with telescopic lenses the cameraman could not get the close-up of the glow. On one side there was the figure of the horse, his four arms stretched at impossible angles as he held himself firm in the crevasse; on the other side of the fire there were the even tinier figures of men, laboring to fit some sort of sling to reach the horse.

For some odd reason having to do with the techniques of recording, the voices came through very plainly, even the heavy, tired breathing of the old horse. Now and then he uttered one of the special horse-words which seemed to be the limit of his vocabulary. He was obviously watching the men, and was firmly persuaded of their friendliness to him. His large, tame, yellow eyes rolled wildly in the light of the searchlight and every time the horse looked down, he seemed to shudder.

Casher O'Neill found this entirely understandable. The bottom of the Hippy Dipsy was nowhere in sight; the horse, even with nothing more than the enlarged fingernails of his middle fingers to help him climb, had managed to get about four of the six kilometers' height of the cliff face behind him.

The voice of a tiger-man sounded clearly from among the shift of men, underpeople and robots who were struggling on the face of the cliff.

"It's a gamble, but not much of a gamble. I weigh six hundred kilos myself, and, do you know, I don't think I've ever had to use my full strength since I was a kitten. I *know* that I can jump across the fire and help that thing be more comfortable. I can even tie a rope around him so that he won't slip and fall after all the work we've done. And the work he's done, too," added the tiger-man grimly. "*Perhaps* I can just take him in my arms and jump back with him. It will be perfectly safe if you have a safety rope around each of us. After all, I never saw a less prehensile creature in my life. You can't call those fingers of his 'fingers.' They look like little boxes of bones, designed for running around and not much good for anything else."

There was a murmur of other voices and then the command of the supervisor. "Go ahead."

No one was prepared for what happened next.

The cameraman got the tiger-man right in the middle of his frame, showing the attachment of one rope around the tiger-man's broad waist. The tiger-man was a modified type whom the authorities had not bothered to put into human cosmetic form. He still had his ears on top of his head, yellow and black fur over his face, huge incisors overlapping his lower jaw and enormous antenna-like whiskers sticking out from his moustache. He must have been thoroughly modified inside, however, because his temperament was calm, friendly and even a little humorous; he must have had a carefully re-done mouth, because the utterance of human speech came to him clearly and without distortion.

He jumped—a mighty jump, right through the top edges of the flame.

The horse saw him.

The horse jumped too, almost in the same moment, also through the top of the flame, going the other way.

The horse had feared the tiger-man more than he did the cliff.

The horse landed right in the group of workers. He tried not to hurt them with his flailing limbs, but he did knock one man—a true man, at that—off the cliff. The man's scream faded as he crashed into the impenetrable darkness below.

The robots were quick. Having no emotions except *on*, *off*, and *high*, they did not get excited. They had the horse trussed and, before the true men and underpeople had ensured their footing, they had signaled the crane operator at the top of the cliff. The horse, his four arms swinging limply, disappeared upward.

The tiger-man jumped back through the flames to the nearer ledge. The picture went off.

In the viewing room, the Hereditary Director Philip Vincent stood up. He stretched, looking around.

Genevieve looked at Casher O'Neill expectantly.

"That's the story," said the Dictator mildly. "Now you solve it."

"Where is the horse now?" said Casher O'Neill.

"In the hospital, of course. My niece can take you to see him."

III

After a short, painful and very thorough peeping of his own mind by the Hereditary Dictator, Casher O'Neill and Genevieve set off for the hospital in which the horse was being kept in bed. The people of Pontoppidan had not known what else to do with him, so they had placed him under strong sedation and were trying to feed him with sugar-water compounds going directly into his veins. Genevieve told Casher that the horse was wasting away.

They walked to the hospital over amethyst pebbles.

Instead of wearing his spacesuit, Casher wore a surface helmet which enriched his oxygen. His hosts had not counted on his getting spells of uncontrollable itching from the sharply reduced atmospheric pressure. He did not dare mention the matter, because he was still hoping to get the green ruby as a weapon in his private war for the liberation of the Twelve Niles from the rule of Colonel Wedder. Whenever the itching became less than excruciating, he enjoyed the walk and the company of the slight, beautiful girl who accompanied him across the fields of jewels to the hospital. (In later years, he sometimes wondered what might have happened. Was the itching a part of his destiny, which saved him for the freedom of the city of Kaheer and the planet Mizzer? Might not the innocent brilliant loveliness of the girl have otherwise tempted him to forswear his duty and stay forever on Pontoppidan?)

The girl wore a new kind of cosmetic for outdoor walking—a warm peachhued powder which let the natural pink of her cheeks show through. Her eyes, he saw, were a living, deep gray; her eyelashes, long; her smile, innocently provocative beyond all ordinary belief. It was a wonder that the Hereditary Dictator had not had to stop duels and murders between young men vying for her favor.

They finally reached the hospital, just as Casher O'Neill thought he could stand it no longer and would have to ask Genevieve for some kind of help or carriage to get indoors and away from the frightful itching.

The building was underground.

The entrance was sumptuous. Diamonds and rubies, the size of building-bricks on Mizzer, had been set to frame the doorway, which was apparently enameled steel. Kuraf at his most lavish had never wasted money on anything like this door-frame. Genevieve saw his glance.

"It did cost a lot of credits. We had to bring a blind artist all the way from Olympia to paint that enamelwork. The poor man. He spent most of his time trying to steal extra gem-stones when he should have known that we pay justly and never allowed anyone to get away with stealing."

"What do you do?" asked Casher O'Neill.

"We cut thieves up in space, just at the edge of the atmosphere. We have more manned boats in orbit than any other planet I know of. Maybe Old North Australia has more, but, then, nobody ever gets close enough to Old North Australia to come back alive and tell."

They went on into the hospital.

A respectful chief surgeon insisted on keeping them in the office and entertaining them with tea and confectionery, when they both wanted to go see the horse; common politeness prohibited their pushing through. Finally they got past the ceremony and into the room in which the horse was kept.

Close up, they could see how much he had suffered. There were cuts and abrasures over almost all of his body. One of his *hooves*—the doctor told them that was the correct name, *hoof*, for the big middle fingernail on which he walked—was split; the doctor had put a cadmium-silver bar through it. The horse lifted his head when they entered, but he saw that they were just more people, not horsey people, so he put his head down, very patiently.

"What's the prospect, doctor?" asked Casher O'Neill, turning away from the animal.

"Could I ask you, sir, a foolish question first?"

Surprised, Casher could only say yes.

"You're an O'Neill. Your uncle is Kuraf. How do you happen to be called 'Casher'?"

"That's simple," laughed Casher. "This is my young-man-name. On Mizzer, everybody gets a baby name, which nobody uses. Then he gets a nickname. Then he gets a young-man-name, based on some characteristic or some friendly joke, until he picks out his career. When he enters his profession, he picks out his own career name. If I liberate Mizzer and overthrow Colonel Wedder, I'll have to think up a suitable career name for myself."

"But why 'Casher,' sir?" persisted the doctor.

"When I was a little boy and people asked me what I wanted, I always asked for cash. I guess that contrasted with my uncle's wastefulness, so they called me Casher."

"But what is cash? One of your crops?"

It was Casher's time to look amazed. "Cash is money. Paper credits. People pass them back and forth when they buy things."

"Here on Pontoppidan, all the money belongs to me. All of it," said Genevieve. "My uncle is trustee for me. But I have never been allowed to touch it or to spend it. It's all just planet business."

The doctor blinked respectfully. "Now this horse, sir, if you will pardon my asking about your name, is a very strange case. Physiologically he is a pure earth type. He is suited only for a vegetable diet, but otherwise he is a very close relative of man. He has a single stomach and a very large cone-shaped heart. That's where the trouble is. The heart is in bad condition. He is dying."

"Dying?" cried Genevieve.

"That's the sad, horrible part," said the doctor. "He is dying but he cannot die. He could go on like this for many years. Perinö wasted enough stroon on this animal to make a planet immortal. Now the animal is worn out but cannot die."

Casher O'Neill let out a long, low, ululating whistle. Everybody in the room jumped. He disregarded them. It was the whistle he had used near the stables, back among the Twelve Niles, when he wanted to call a horse.

The horse knew it. The large head lifted. The eyes rolled at him so imploringly that he expected tears to fall from them, even though he was pretty sure that horses could not lachrymate.

He squatted on the floor, close to the horse's head, with a hand on its mane.

"Quick," he murmured to the surgeon. "Get me a piece of sugar and an underperson-telepath. The underperson-telepath must not be of carnivorous origin."

The doctor looked stupid. He snapped "Sugar" at an assistant, but he squatted down next to Casher O'Neill and said, "You will have to repeat that about an underperson. This is not an underperson hospital at all. We have very few of them here. The horse is here only by command of His Excellency Philip Vincent, who said that the horse of Perinö should be given the best of all possible care. He even told me," said the doctor, "that if anything wrong happened to this horse, I would ride patrol for it for the next eighty years. So I'll do what I can. Do you find me too talkative? Some people do. What kind of an underperson do you want?"

"I need," said Casher, very calmly, "a telepathic underperson, both to find out what this horse wants and to tell the horse that I am here to help him. Horses are vegetarians and they do not like meat-eaters. Do you have a vegetarian underperson around the hospital?"

"We used to have some squirrel-men," said the chief surgeon, "but when we changed the air circulating system the squirrel-men went away with the old equipment. I think they went to a mine. We have tiger-men, cat-men, and my secretary is a wolf."

"Oh, no!" said Casher O'Neill. "Can you imagine a sick horse confiding in a wolf?"

"It's no more than you are doing," said the surgeon, very softly, glancing up to see if Genevieve were in hearing range, and apparently judging that she was not. "The Hereditary Dictators here sometimes cut suspicious guests to pieces on their way off the planet. That is, unless the guests are licensed, regular traders. You are not. You might be a spy, planning to rob us. How do I know? I wouldn't give a diamond chip for your chances of being alive next week. What do you want to do about the horse? That might please the Dictator. And *you* might live."

Casher O'Neill was so staggered by the confidence of the surgeon that he squatted there thinking about himself, not about the patient. The horse licked him, seemingly sensing that he needed solace.

The surgeon had an idea. "Horses and dogs used to go together, didn't they, back in the old days of Man-home, when all the people lived on planet Earth?"

"Of course," said Casher. "We still run them together in hunts on Mizzer, but under these new laws of the Instrumentality we've run out of underpeople-criminals to hunt."

"I have a good dog," said the chief surgeon. "She talks pretty well, but she is so sympathetic that she upsets the patients by loving them too much. I have her down in the second underbasement tending the dish-sterilizing machinery."

"Bring her up," said Casher in a whisper.

He remembered that he did not need to whisper about this, so he stood up and spoke to Genevieve:

"They have found a good dog-telepath who may reach through to the mind of the horse. It may give us the answer."

She put her hand on his forearm gently, with the approbatory gesture of a princess. Her fingers dug into his flesh. Was she wishing him well against her uncle's habitual treachery, or was this merely the impulse of a kind young girl who knew nothing of the way the world was run?

IV

The interview went extremely well.

The dog-woman was almost perfectly humaniform. She looked like a tired, cheerful, worn-out old woman, not valuable enough to be given the life-prolonging santaclara drug called *stroon*. Work had been her life and she had had plenty of it. Casher O'Neill felt a twinge of envy when he realized that happiness goes by the petty chances of life and not by the large destiny. This dog-woman, with her haggard face and her string gray hair, had more love, happiness and sympathy than Kuraf had found with his pleasures, Colonel

Wedder with his powers, or himself with his crusade. Why did life do that? Was there no justice, ever? Why should a worn-out worthless old underwoman be happy when he was not?

"Never mind," she said, "you'll get over it and then you will be happy."

"Over what?" he said. "I didn't say anything."

"I'm not going to say it," she retorted, meaning that she was telepathic. "You're a prisoner of yourself. Some day you will escape to unimportance and happiness. You're a good man. You're trying to save yourself, but you really *like* this horse."

"Of course I do," said Casher O'Neill. "He's a brave old horse, climbing out of that hell to get back to people."

When he said the word *hell* her eyes widened, but she said nothing. In his mind he saw the sign of a fish scrawled on a dark wall and he felt her think at him, *So you too know something of the "dark wonderful knowledge" which is not yet to be revealed to all mankind?*

He thought a *cross* back at her and then turned his thinking to the horse, lest her telepathy be monitored and strange punishments await them both.

She spoke in words, "Shall we link?"

"Link," he said.

Genevieve stepped up. Her clear-cut, pretty, sensitive face was alight with excitement. "Could I—could I be cut in?"

"Why not?" said the dog-woman, glancing at him. He nodded. The three of them linked hands and then the dog-woman put her left hand on the forehead of the old horse.

The sand splashed beneath their feet as they ran toward Kaheer. The delicious pressure of a man's body was on their backs. The red sky of Mizzer gleamed over them. There came the shout:

"I'm a horse, I'm a horse, I'm a horse!"

"You're from Mizzer," thought Casher O'Neill, "from Kaheer itself!"

"I don't know names," thought the horse, "but you're from my land. The land, the good land."

"What are you doing here?"

"Dying," thought the horse. "Dying for hundreds and thousands of sundowns. The old one brought me. No riding, no running, no people. Just the old one and the small ground. I have been dying since I came here."

Casher O'Neill got a glimpse of Perinö sitting and watching the horse, unconscious of the cruelty and loneliness which he had inflicted on his large pet by making it immortal and then giving it no work to do.

"Do you know what dying is?"

Thought the horse promptly: "Certainly. No-horse."

"Do you know what life is?"

"Yes. Being a horse."

"I'm not a horse," thought Casher O'Neill, "but I am alive."

"Don't complicate things," thought the horse at him, though Casher realized it was his own mind and not the horse's which supplied the words.

"Do you want to die?"

"To no-horse? Yes, if this room, forever, is the end of things."

"What would you like better?" thought Genevieve, and her thoughts were like a cascade of newly-minted silver coins falling into all their minds: brilliant, clean, bright, innocent.

The answer was quick: "Dirt beneath my hooves, and wet air again, and a man on my back."

The dog-woman interrupted him: "Dear horse, you know me?"

"You're a dog," thought the horse. "Goo-oo-oo-ood dog!"

"Right," thought the happy old slattern, "and I can tell

these people how to take care of you. Sleep now, and when you waken you will be on the way to happiness."

She thought the command *sleep* so powerfully at the old horse that Casher O'Neill and Genevieve both started to fall unconscious and had to be caught by the hospital attendants.

As they re-gathered their wits, she was finishing her commands to the surgeon. "—and put about 40% supplementary oxygen into the air. He'll have to have a real person to ride him, but some of your orbiting sentries would rather ride a horse up their than do nothing. You can't repair the heart. Don't try it. Hypnosis will take care of the sand of Mizzer. Just load his mind with one or two of the drama-cubes packed full of desert adventure. Now, don't you worry about me. I'm not going to give you any more suggestions. People-man, you!" She laughed. "You can forgive dogs anything, except for being right. It makes you feel inferior for a few minutes. Never mind. I'm going back downstairs to my dishes. I love them, I really do. Good-bye, you pretty thing," she said to Genevieve. "And good-bye, wanderer! Good luck to you," she said to Casher O'Neill. "You will remain miserable as long as you seek justice, but when you give up, righteousness will come to you and you will be happy. Don't worry. You're young and it won't hurt you to suffer a few more years. Youth is an extremely curable disease, isn't it?"

She gave them a full curtsy, like one Lady of the Instrumentality saying good-bye to another. Her wrinkled old face was lit up with smiles, in which happiness was mixed with a tiniest bit of playful mockery.

"Don't mind me, boss," she said to the surgeon. "Dishes, here I come." She swept out of the room.

"See what I mean?" said the surgeon. "She's so horribly *happy!* How can anyone run a hospital if a dishwasher gets all over the place, making people happy? We'd be out of jobs. Her ideas were good, though."

They were. They worked. Down to the last letter of the dog-woman's instructions.

There was argument from the council. Casher O'Neill went along to see them in session.

One councillor, Bashnack, was particularly vociferous in objecting to any action concerning the horse. "Sire," he cried, "sire! We don't even know the name of the animal! I must protest this action, when we don't know—"

"That we don't," assented Philip Vincent. "But what does a name have to do with it?"

"The horse has no identity, not even the identity of an animal. It is just a pile of meat left over from the estate of Perinö. We should kill the horse and eat the meat ourselves. Or, if we do not want to eat the meat, then we should sell it off-planet. There are plenty of peoples around here who would pay a pretty price for genuine earth meat. Pay no attention to me, sire! You are the Hereditary Dictator and I am nothing. I have no power, no property, nothing. I am at your mercy. All I can tell you is to follow your own best interests. I have only a voice. You cannot reproach me for using my voice when I am trying to help you, sire, can you? That's all I am doing, helping you. If you spend any credits at all on this animal you will be doing wrong, wrong, wrong. We are not a rich planet. We have to pay for expensive defenses just in order to stay alive. We cannot even afford to pay for air that our children can go out and play. And you want to spend money on a horse which cannot even talk! I tell you, sire, this council is going to vote against you, just to protect your own interests and the interests of the Honorable Genevieve as Eventual Title-holder of all Pontoppidan. You are not going to get away with this, sire! We are helpless before your power, but we will insist on advising you—"

"Hear! Hear!" cried several of the councillors, not the

least dismayed by the slight frown of the Hereditary Dictator.

"I will take the word," said Philip Vincent himself.

Several had had their hands raised, asking for the floor. One obstinate man kept his hand up even when the Dictator announced his intention to speak. Philip Vincent took note of him, too:

"You can talk when I'm through, if you want to."

He looked calmly around the room, smiled imperceptibly at his niece, gave Casher O'Neill the briefest of nods, and then announced:

"Gentlemen, it's not the horse which is on trial. It's Pontoppidan. It's we who are trying ourselves. And before whom are we trying ourselves, gentlemen? Each of us is before that most awful of courts, his own conscience.

"If we kill that horse, gentlemen, we will not be doing the horse a great wrong. He is an old animal, and I do not think that he will mind dying very much, now that he is away from the ordeal of loneliness which he feared more than death. After all, he has already had his great triumph— the climb up the cliff of gems, the jump across the volcanic vent, the rescue by people whom he wanted to find. The horse has done so well that he is really beyond us. We can help him, a little, or we can hurt him, a little; beside the immensity of his accomplishment, we cannot really do very much either way.

"No, gentlemen, we are not judging the case of the horse. We are judging space. What happens to a man when he moves out into the Big Nothing? Do we leave Old Earth behind? Why did civilization fall? Will it fall again? Is civilization a gun or a blaster or a laser or a rocket? Is it even a planoforming ship or a pinlighter at his work? You know as well as I do, gentlemen, that civilization is not good-bye and good, good luck to you. My uncle expects us."

Together they went back into the palace.

* * *

Another memory was the farewell to Philip Vincent, the Hereditary Dictator of Pontoppidan. The calm, clean-shaven, ruddy, well-fleshed face looked at him with benign regard. Casher O'Neill felt more respect for this man when he realized that ruthlessness is often the price of peace, and vigilance the price of wealth.

"You're a clever young man. A very clever young man. You may win back the power of your Uncle Kuraf."

"I don't want *that* power!" cried Casher O'Neill.

"I have advice for you," said the Hereditary Dictator, "and it is good advice or I would not be here to give it. I have learned the political arts well: otherwise I would not be alive. Do not refuse power. Just take it and use it wisely. Do not hide from your wicked uncle's name. Obliterate it. Take the name yourself and rule so well that, in a few decades, no one will remember your uncle. Just you. You are young. You can't win now. But it is in your fate to grow and to triumph. I know it. I am good at these things. I have given you your weapon. I am not tricking you. It is packed safely and you may leave with it."

Casher O'Neill was breathing softly, believing it all, and trying to think of words to thank the stout, powerful older man when the dictator added, with a little laugh in his voice:

"Thank you, too, for saving me money. You've lived up to your name, Casher."

"Saved you money?"

"The alfalfa. The horse wanted alfalfa."

"Oh, that idea!" said Casher O'Neill. "It was obvious. I don't deserve much credit for that."

"*I* didn't think of it," said the Hereditary Dictator, "and my staff didn't either. We're not stupid. That shows you are bright. You realized that Perinö must have had a food converter to keep the horse alive in the Hippy Dipsy. All we did was set it to alfalfa and we saved ourselves the cost of a shipload of horse food twice a year. We're glad to save that credit. We're well off here, but we don't like to waste things. You may bow to me now, and leave."

Casher O'Neill had done so, with one last glance at the lovely Genevieve, standing fragile and beautiful beside her uncle's chair.

His last memory was very recent.

He had paid two hundred thousand credits for it, right on this liner. He had found the Stop-Captain, bored now that the ship was in flight and the Go-Captain had taken over.

"Can you get me a telepathic fix on a horse?"

"What's a horse?" said the Go-Captain. "Where is it? Do you want to pay for it?"

"A horse," said Casher O'Neill patiently, "is an unmodified earth animal. Not underpeople. A big one, but quite intelligent. This one is in orbit right around Pontoppidan. And I will pay the usual price."

"A million Earth credits," said the Stop-Captain.

"Ridiculous!" cried Casher O'Neill.

They settled on two hundred thousand credits for a good fix and ten thousand for the use of the ship's equipment even if there were failure. It was not a failure. The technician was a snake-man: he was deft, cool, and superb at his job. In only a few minutes he passed the headset to Casher O'Neill, saying politely, "This is it, I think."

It was. He had reached right into the horse's mind.

The endless sands of Mizzer swam before Casher O'Neill. The long lines of the Twelve Niles converged in the distance. He galloped steadily and powerfully. There were other horses nearby, other riders, other things, but he himself was conscious only of the beat of the hooves against the strong moist sand, the firmness of the appreciative rider upon his back. Dimly, as in a hallucination, Casher O'Neill could also see the little orbital ship in which the old horse cantered in mid-air, with an amused cadet sitting on his back. Up there, with no weight, the old worn-out heart would be good for many, many years. Then he saw the horse's paradise again. The flash of hooves threatened to overtake him, but he outran them all. There was the expectation of a stable at the end, a rubdown, good succulent green food, and the glimpse of a filly in the morning.

The horse of Pontoppidan felt extremely wise. He had trusted *people*—people, the source of all kindness, all cruelty, all power among the stars. And the people had been good. The horse felt very much horse again. Casher felt the old body course along the river's edge like a dream of power, like a completion of service, like an ultimate fulfillment of companionship.

Part Two

I

"At two seventy-five in the morning," said the Administrator to Casher O'Neill, "you will kill this girl with a knife. At two seventy-seven, a fast groundcar will pick you up and bring you back here. Then the power cruiser will be yours. Is that a deal?"

He held out his hand as if he wanted Casher O'Neill to shake it then and there, making some kind of an oath or bargain.

Casher did not slight the man, so he picked up his glass and said, "Let's drink to the deal, first!"

The Administrator's quick, restless, darting eyes looked Casher up and down very suspiciously. The warm sea-wet air blew through the room. The Administrator seemed wary, suspicious, alert, but underneath his slight hostility there was another emotion, of which Casher could perceive just the edge. Fatigue with its roots in bottomless despair: despair set deep in irrecoverable fatigue?

That other emotion, which Casher could barely discern, was very strange indeed. On all his voyages back and forth through the inhabited worlds, Casher had met many odd types of men and women. He had never seen anything like this Administrator before—brilliant, erratic, boastful. His title was "Mr. Commissioner" and he was an ex-Lord of the Instrumentality on this planet of Henriada, where the population had dropped from six hundred million persons down to some forty thousand. Indeed, local government had disappeared into limbo, and this odd man, with the title of "Administrator," was the only law and civil authority which the planet knew.

Nevertheless, he had a surplus power cruiser and Casher O'Neill was determined to get that cruiser as a part of his long plot to return to his home planet of Mizzer and to unseat the usurper, Colonel Wedder.

The Administrator stared sharply, wearily at Casher and then he, too, lifted his glass. The green twilight colored his liquor and made it seem like some strange poison. It was only Earth-byegarr, though a little on the strong side.

With a sip, only a sip, the older man relaxed a little. "You may be out to trick me, young man. You may think that I am an old fool running an abandoned planet. You may even be thinking that killing this girl is some kind of a crime. It is not a crime at all. I am the Administrator of Henriada and I have ordered that girl killed every year for the last eighty years. She isn't even a girl, to start with. Just an underperson. Some kind of an animal turned into a domestic servant. I can even appoint you a deputy sheriff. Or chief of detectives. That might be better. I haven't had a chief of detectives for a hundred years and more. You are my chief of detectives. Go in tomorrow. The house is not hard to find. It's the biggest and best house left on this planet. Go in tomorrow morning. Ask for her master and be sure that you use the correct title, 'Mister and Owner Murray Madigan.' The robots will tell you to keep out. If you persist, she will come to the door. That's when you will stab her through the heart, right there in the doorway. My ground-car will race up one metric minute later. You jump in and come back here. We've been through this before. Why don't you agree? Don't you know who I am?"

"I know perfectly well"—Casher O'Neill smiled—"who you are, Mr. Commissioner and Administrator. You are the honorable Rankin Meiklejohn, once of Earth Two. After all, the Instrumentality itself gave me a permit to land on this planet on private business. They knew who *I* was, too, and what I wanted. There's something funny about all this. Why should you give me a power cruiser—the best ship, you yourself say, in your whole fleet—just for killing one modified animal which looks and talks like a girl? Why me? Why the visitor? Why the man from off-world? Why should you care whether this particular underperson is killed or not? If you've given the order for her death eighty times in eighty years, why hasn't it been carried out long ago? Mind you, Mr. Administrator, I'm not saying no. I want that cruiser. I want it very much indeed. But what's the deal? What's the trick? Is it the house you want?"

"Beauregard? No, I don't want Beauregard. Old Madigan can rot in it for all that I care. It's between Ambiloxi and Mottile, on the Gulf of Esperanza. You can't miss it. The road is good. You could drive yourself there."

"What is it, then?" Casher's voice had an edge of persistence to it.

The Administrator's response was singular indeed. He filled his huge inhaler-glass with the potent byegarr. He stared over the full glass at Casher O'Neill as if he were an enemy. He drained the glass. Casher knew that that much liquor, taken suddenly, could kill the normal human being.

The Administrator did not fall over dead.

He did not even become noticeably more drunk.

His face turned red and his eyes almost popped out, as the harsh 160-proof liquor took effect, but he still did not say anything. He just stared at Casher. Casher, who had learned in his long exile to play many games, just stared back.

The Administrator broke first.

He leaned forward and burst into a bird-like shriek of laughter. The laughter went on and on until it seemed that the man had hogged all the merriment in the galaxy. Casher snorted a little laugh along with the man, more out of nervous reflex than anything else, but he waited for the Administrator to stop laughing.

The Administrator finally got control of himself. With a broad grin and a wink at Casher, he poured himself four fingers more of the byegarr into his glass, drank it down as if he had had a sip of cream, and then—only very slightly unsteady—stood up, came over, and patted Casher on the shoulder.

"You're a smart boy, my lad. I'm cheating you. I don't care whether the power cruiser is there or not. I'm giving you something which has no value at all to me. Who's ever going to take a power cruiser off this planet? It's ruined. It's abandoned. And so am I. Go ahead. You can have the cruiser. For nothing. Just take it. Free. Unconditionally."

This time it was Casher who leaped to his feet and stared down into the face of the feverish, wanton little man.

"Thank you, Mr. Administrator!" he cried, trying to catch the hand of the Administrator so as to seal the deal.

Rankin Meiklejohn looked awfully sober for a man with that much liquor in him. He held his right hand behind his back and would not shake.

"You can have the cruiser all right. No terms. No conditions. No deal. It's yours. *But kill that girl first!* Just as a favor to me. I've been a good host. I like you. I want to do you a favor. Do me one. Kill that girl. At two seventy-five in the morning. Tomorrow."

"Why?" asked Casher, his voice loud and cold, trying to wring some sense out of the chattering man.

"Just—just—just because I say so. . . ." stammered the Administrator.

"Why?" asked Casher, cold and loud again.

The liquor suddenly took over inside the Administrator. He groped back for the arm of his chair, sat down suddenly and then looked up at Casher. He was very drunk indeed. The strange emotion, the elusive fatigue-despair, had vanished from his face. He spoke straightforwardly. Only the excessive care of his articulation would have shown a passer-by that he was drunk.

"Because, you fool," said Meiklejohn, "those people, more than eighty in eighty years, that I have sent to Beauregard with orders to kill the girl. Those people—" he repeated, and stopped speaking, clamping his lips together.

"What happened to them?" asked Casher calmly and persuasively.

The Administrator grinned again and seemed to be on the edge of one of his wild laughs.

"What happened?" shouted Casher at him.

"I don't know," said the Administrator. "For the life of me, I don't know. Not one of them ever came back."

"What happened to them? Did she kill them?" cried Casher.

"How would I know?" said the drunken man, getting visibly more sleepy.

"Why didn't you report it?"

This seemed to rouse the Administrator. "Report that one little girl had stopped me, the planetary Administrator? Just one little girl, and not even a human being! They would have sent help, and laughed at me. By the Bell, young man, I've been laughed at enough! I need no help from outside. You're going in there tomorrow morning. At two seventy-five, with a knife. And a groundcar waiting."

He stared fixedly at Casher and then suddenly fell asleep in his chair. Casher called to the robots to show him to his room; they tended to the master as well.

II

The next morning at two seventy-five sharp, nothing happened. Casher walked down the baroque corridor, looking into beautiful barren rooms. All the doors were open.

Through one door he heard a sick, deep bubbling snore.

It was the Administrator, sure enough. He lay twisted on his bed. A small nursing machine was beside him, her white enameled body only slightly rusty. She held up a mechanical hand for silence and somehow managed to make the gesture seem light, delicate and pretty, even from a machine.

Casher walked lightly back to his own room, where he ordered hotcakes, bacon and coffee. He studied a tornado through the armored glass of his window, while the robots prepared his food. The elastic trees clung to the earth with a fury which matched the fury of the wind. The trunk of the tornado reached like the nose of a mad elephant down into the gardens, but the flora fought back. A few animals whipped upward and out of sight. The tornado then came straight for the house, but did not damange it outside of making a lot of noise.

"We have two or three hundred of those a day," said a butler robot. "That is why we store all space-craft underground and have no weather machines. It would cost more, the people said, to make this planet livable than the planet could possibly yield. The radio and news are in the library,

42

sir. I do not think that the honorable Rankin Meiklejohn will wake until evening, say seven-fifty or eight o'clock."

"Can I go out?"

"Why not, sir? You are a true man. You can do what you wish."

"I mean, is it safe for me to go out?"

"Oh, no, sir! The wind would tear you apart or carry you away."

"Don't people ever go out?"

"Yes, sir. With groundcars or with automatic body armor. I have been told that if it weighs fifty tons or better, the person inside is safe. I would not know, sir. As you see, I am a robot. I was made here, though my brain was formed on Earth Two, and I have never been outside this house."

Casher looked at the robot. This one seemed unusually talkative. He chanced the opportunity of getting some more information.

"Have you ever heard of Beauregard?"

"Yes, sir. It is the best house on this planet. I have heard people say that it is the most solid building on Henriada. It belongs to the Mister and Owner Murray Madigan. He is an Old North Australian, a renunciant who left his home planet and came here when Henriada was a busy world. He brought all his wealth with him. The underpeople and robots say that it is a wonderful place on the inside."

"Have you seen it?"

"Oh, no, sir, I have never left this building."

"Does the man Madigan ever come here?"

The robot seemed to be trying to laugh, but did not succeed. He answered, very unevenly, "Oh, no, sir. He never goes anywhere."

"Can you tell me anything about the female who lives with him?"

"No, sir," said the robot.

"Do you know anything about her?"

"Sir, it is not that. I know a great deal about her."

"Why can't you talk about her, then?"

"I have been commanded not to, sir."

"I am," said Casher O'Neill, "a true human being. I herewith countermand those orders. Tell me about her."

The robot's voice became formal and cold. "The orders cannot be countermanded, sir."

"Why not?" snapped Casher. "Are they the Administrator's?"

"No, sir."

"Whose, then?"

"Hers," said the robot softly, and left the room.

III

Casher O'Neill spent the rest of the day trying to get information; he obtained very little.

The Deputy Administrator was a young man who hated his chief.

When Casher, who dined with him—the two of them having a poorly-cooked state luncheon in a dining room which would have seated five hundred people—tried to come to the point by asking bluntly, "What do you know about Murray Madigan?" he got an answer which was blunt to the point of incivility.

"Nothing."

"You never heard of him?" cried Casher.

"Keep your troubles to yourself, mister visitor," said the Deputy Administrator. "I've got to stay on this planet long enough to get promoted off. You can leave. You shouldn't have come."

"I have," said Casher, "an all-world pass from the Instrumentality."

"All right," said the young man, "that shows that you are more important than I am. Let's not discuss the matter. Do you like your lunch?"

Casher had learned diplomacy in his childhood, when he was the heir apparent to the Dictatorship of Mizzer. When his horrible uncle, Kuraf, lost the rulership, Casher had approved of the coup by the Colonels Wedder and Gibna; but now Wedder was supreme and enforcing a period of terror and virtue. Casher thus knew courts and ceremony, big talk and small talk, and on this occasion, he let the small talk do. The young Deputy Administrator had only one ambition, to get off the planet Henriada and never to see or hear of Rankin Meiklejohn again.

Casher could understand the point.

Only one curious thing happened during dinner.

Toward the end, Casher slipped in the question, very informally: "Can underpeople give orders to robots?"

"Of course," said the young man. "That's one of the reasons we use underpeople. They have more initiative. They amplify our orders to robots on many occasions."

Casher smiled. "I didn't mean it quite that way. Could an underperson give an order to a robot which a real human being could not then countermand?"

The young man started to answer, even though his mouth was full of food. He was not a very polished young man. Suddenly he stopped chewing and his eyes grew wide. Then, with his mouth half full, he said: "You are trying to talk about this planet, I guess. You can't help it. You're on the track. Stay on the track, then. Maybe you will get out of it alive. I refuse to get mixed up with it, with you, with him and his hateful schemes. All I want to do is to leave when my time comes."

The young man resumed chewing, his eyes fixed steadfastly on his plate.

Before Casher could pass off the matter by making some casual remark, the butler robot stopped behind him and leaned over.

"Honorable sir, I heard your question. May I answer it?"

"Of course," said Casher, softly.

"The answer, sir," said the butler-robot, softly but clearly, "to your question is *no, no, never*. That is the general rule of the civilized worlds. But on this planet of Henriada, sir, the answer is *yes*."

"Why?" asked Casher.

"It is my duty, sir," said the robot butler, "to recommend to you this dish of fresh artichokes. I am not authorized to deal with other matters."

"Thank you," said Casher, straining a little to keep himself looking imperturbable.

Nothing much happened that night, except that Meiklejohn got up long enough to get drunk all over again. Though he invited Casher to come and drink with him, he never seriously discussed the girl except for one outburst.

"Leave it till tomorrow. Fair and square. Open and above-board. Frank and honest. That's me. I'll take you around Beauregard myself. You'll see it's easy. A knife, eh? A traveled young man like you would know what to do with a knife. And a little girl, too. Not very big. Easy job. Don't give it another thought. Would you like some apple juice in your byegarr?"

Casher had taken three contraintoxicant pills before going to drink with the ex-Lord, but even at that, he could not keep up with Meiklejohn. He accepted the dilution of apple juice gravely, gracefully, and gratefully.

The little tornadoes stamped around the house. Meiklejohn, now launched into some drunken story of ancient injustices which had been done to him on other worlds, paid no attention to them. In the middle of the night, past nine-fifty in the evening, Casher woke alone in his chair, very stiff and uncomfortable. The robots must have had standing instructions concerning the Administrator, and had apparently taken him off to bed. Casher walked wearily to his own room, cursed the thundering ceiling and went to sleep again.

IV

The next day was very different indeed.

The Administrator was as sober, brisk and charming as if he had never taken a drink in his life.

He had the robots call Casher to join him at breakfast and said, by way of greeting, "I'll wager you thought I was drunk last night."

"Well . . ." said Casher.

"Planet fever. That's what it was. Planet fever. A bit of alcohol keeps it from developing too far. Let's see. It's three-sixty now. Could you be ready to leave by four?"

Casher frowned at his watch, which had the conventional twenty-four hours.

The Administrator saw the glance and apologized. "Sorry! My fault, a thousand times. I'll get you a metric watch right away. Ten hours a day, a hundred minutes an hour. We're very progressive here on Henriada."

He clapped his hands and ordered that a watch be taken to Casher's room, along with the watch-repairing robot to adjust it to Casher's body rhythms.

"Four, then" he said, rising briskly from the table. "Dress for a trip by groundcar. The servants will show you how."

There was a man already waiting in Casher's room. He looked like a plump, wise ancient Hindu, as shown in the archaeology books. He bowed pleasantly and said, "My name is Gosigo. I am a forgetty, settled on this planet, but for this day I am your guide and driver from this place to the mansion of Beauregard."

Forgetties were barely above underpeople in status. They were persons convicted of various major crimes, to whom the courts of the worlds, or the Instrumentality, had allowed total amnesia instead of death or some punishment worse than death, such as the planet Shayol.

Casher looked at him curiously. The man did not carry with him the permanent air of bewilderment which Casher had noticed in many forgetties. Gosigo saw the glance and interpreted it.

"I'm well enough, now, sir. And I am strong enough to break your back if I had the orders to do it."

"You mean, damage my spine? What a hostile, unpleasant thing to do!" said Casher. "Anyhow, I rather think I could kill you first if you tried it. Whatever gave you such an idea?"

"The Administrator is always threatening people that he will have me do it to them."

"Have you ever really broken anybody's back?" asked Casher, looking Gosigo over very carefully and re-judging him. The man, though shorter than Casher, was luxuriously muscled; like many plump men, he looked pleasant on the outside but could be very formidable to an enemy.

Gosigo smiled briefly, almost happily. "Well, no, not exactly."

"Why haven't you? Does the Administrator always countermand his own orders? I shoul think that he would sometimes be too drunk to remember to do it?"

"It's not that . . ." said Gosigo.

"Why don't you, then?"

"I have other orders," said Gosigo, rather hesitantly. "Like the orders I have today. One set from the Administrator, one set from the Deputy Administrator, and a third set from an outside source."

"Who's the outside source?"

"She has told me not to explain just yet."

Casher stood stock still. "Do you mean who I think you mean?"

Gosigo nodded very slowly, pointing at the ventilator as though it might have a microphone in it.

"Can you tell me what your orders are?"

"Oh, certainly. The Administrator has told me to drive both himself and you to Beauregard, to take you to the door, to watch you stab the undergirl, and to call the second groundcar to your rescue. The Deputy Administrator has told me to take you to Beauregard and to let you do as you please, bringing you back here by way of Ambiloxi if you happen to come out of Mister Murray's house alive."

"And the other orders?"

"To close the door upon you when you enter and to think of you no more in this life, because you will be very happy."

"Are you crazy?" cried Casher.

"I am a forgetty," said Gosigo, with some dignity, "but I am not insane"

"Whose orders are you going to obey then?"

Gosigo smiled a warmly human smile at him. "Doesn't that depend on you, sir, and not on me? Do I look like a man who's going to kill you soon?"

"No, you don't," said Casher.

"Do you think what you look like to me?" went on Gosigo, with a purr. "Do you really think that I would help you if I thought that you would kill a small girl?"

"You know it!" cried Casher, feeling his face go white.

"Who doesn't?" said Gosigo. "What else have we got to talk about, here on Henriada? Let me help you on with these clothes, so that you will at least survive the ride." With this he handed shoulder padding and padded helmet to Casher, who began to put on the garments, very clumsily.

Gosigo helped him.

When Casher was fully dressed, he thought that he had never dressed this elaborately for space itself. The world of Henriada must be a tumultuous place if people needed this kind of clothing to make a short trip.

Gosigo had put on the same kind of clothes.

He looked at Casher in a friendly manner, with an arch smile which came close to humor. "Look at me, honorable visitor. Do I remind you of anybody?"

Casher looked honestly and carefully, and then said, "No, you don't."

The man's face fell. "It's a game," he said. "I can't help trying to find out who I really am. Am I a Lord of the Instrumentality who has betrayed his trust? Am I a scientist who twisted knowledge into unimaginable wrong? Am I a dictator so foul that even the Instrumentality, which usually leaves things alone, had to step in and wipe me out? Here I am, healthy, wise, alert. I have the name Gosigo on this planet. Perhaps I am a mere native of this planet, who has committed a local crime. I am triggered. If anyone ever did tell me my true name or my actual past, I have been conditioned to shriek loud, fall unconscious, and forget anything which might be said on such an occasion. People told me that I must have chosen this instead of death. Maybe. Death sometimes looks tidy to a forgetty."

"Have you ever screamed and fainted?"

"I don't even know *that*," said Gosigo, "no more than you know where you are going this very day."

Casher was tied to the man's mystifications, so he did not let himself be provoked into a useless show of curiosity. Inquisitve about the forgetty himself, he asked:

"Does it hurt . . . does it hurt to be a forgetty?"

"No," said Gosigo, "it doesn't hurt, no more than you will."

Gosigo stared suddenly at Casher. His voice changed tone and became at least one octave higher. He clapped his hands to his face and panted through his hands as if he would never speak again.

"But—Oh! The fear—the eerie, dreary fear of *being me . . . !*"

He still stared at Casher.

Quieting down at last, he pulled his hands away from his face, as if by sheer force, and said in an almost-normal voice, "Shall we get on with out trip?"

Gosigo led the way out into the bare bleak corridor. A perceptible wind was blowing through it, though there was no sign of an open window or door. They followed a majestic staircase, with steps so broad that Casher had to keep changing pace on them, all the way down to the bottom of the building. This must, at some time, have been a formal reception hall. Now it was full of cars.

Curious cars.

Land vehicles of a kind which Casher had never seen before. They looked a little bit like the ancient "fighting tanks" which he had seen in pictures. They also looked a little like submarines of a singularly short and ugly shape. They had high spiked wheels, but their most complicated feature was a set of giant corkscrews, four on each side, attached to the car by intricate yet operational appartus. Since Casher had been landed right into the palace by planoform, he had never had occasion to go outside among the tornadoes of Henriada.

The Administrator was waiting, wearing a coverall on which was stenciled his insignia of rank.

Casher gave him a polite bow. He glanced down at the handsome metric wristwatch which Gosigo had strapped on his wrist, outside the coverall. It read: 3:95.

Casher bowed to Rankin Meiklejohn and said, "I'm ready, sir, if you are."

"Watch him!" whispered Gosigo, half a step behind Casher.

The Administrator said, "Might as well be going." The man's voice trembled.

Casher stood polite, alert, immobile. Was this danger? Was this foolishness? Could the Administrator already be drunk again?

Casher watched the Administrator carefully but quietly, waiting for the older man to precede him into the nearest groundcar, which had its door standing opened.

Nothing happened, except that the Administrator began to turn pale.

There must have been six or eight people present. The others must have seen the same sort of thing before, because they showed no sign of curiosity or bewilderment. The Administrator began to tremble. Casher could see it, even through the bulk of the travelwear. The man's hands shook.

The Administrator said, in a high nervous voice: "Your knife. You have it with you?"

Casher nodded.

"Let me see it," said the Administrator.

Casher reached down to his boot and brought out the beautiful, superbly-balanced knife. Before he could stand erect, he felt the clamp of Gosigo's heavy fingers on his shoulder.

"Master," said Gosigo to Meiklejohn, "tell your visitor to put his weapon away. It is not allowed for any of us to show weapons in your presence."

Casher tried to squirm out of the heavy grip without losing his balance or his dignity. He found that Gosigo was knowledgeable about karate too. The forgetty held ground, even when the two men waged an immobile, invisible sort of wrestling match, the leverage of Casher's shoulder working its way hither and yon against the strong grip of Gosigo's powerful hand.

The Administrator ended it. He said, "Put away your knife. . . ." in that high funny voice of his.

The watch had almost reached 4:00, but no one had yet gotten into the car.

Gosigo spoke again, and when he did there was a contemptuous laugh from the Deputy Administrator, who had stood by in ordinary indoor clothes.

"Master, isn't it time for 'one for the road'?"

"Of course, of course," chattered the Administrator. He began breathing almost normally again.

"Join me," he said to Casher, "it's a local custom."

Casher had let his knife slip back into his bootsheath. When the knife dropped out of sight, Gosigo released his shoulder; he now stood facing the Administrator and rubbed his bruised shoulder. He said nothing, but shook his head gently, showing that he did not want a drink.

One of the robots brought the Administrator a glass, which appeared to contain at least a liter and a half of water. The Administrator said, very politely, "Sure you won't share it?"

This close, Casher could smell the reek of it. It was pure byegarr, and at least 160° proof. He shook his head again, firmly but also politely.

The Administrator lifted the glass.

Casher could see the muscles of the man's throat work as the liquid went down. He could hear the man breathing heavily between swallows. The white liquid went lower and lower in the gigantic glass.

At last it was all gone.

The Administrator cocked his head sidewise and said to Casher in a parrot-like voice, "Well, toodle-oo!"

"What do you mean, sir?" asked Casher.

The Administrator had a pleasant glow on his face.

Casher was surprised that the man was not dead after that
big and sudden a drink.

"I just mean, g'bye. I'm—not—feeling—well."

With that he fell straight forward, as stiff as a rock tower.
One of the servants, perhaps another forgetty, caught him
before he hit the ground.

"Does he always do this?" asked Casher of the miserable
and contemptuous Deputy Administrator.

"Oh, no," said the Deputy. "Only at times like these."

"What do you mean, 'like these'?"

"When he sends one more armed man against the girl at
Beauregard. They never come back. You won't come back,
either. You could have left earlier, but you can't now. Go
along and try to kill the girl. I'll see you here about 5:25 if
you succeed. As a matter of fact, if you come back at all,
I'll try to wake *him* up. But you won't come back. Good
luck. I suppose that's what you need. Good luck."

Casher shook hands with the man without removing his
gloves. Gosigo had already climbed into the driver's seat of
the machine and was testing the electric engines. The big
corkscrews began to plunge down, but before they touched
the floor, Gosigo had reversed them and thrown them back
into the "up" position.

The people in the room ran for cover as Casher entered
the machine, though there was no immediate danger in
sight. Two of the human servants dragged the Administrator
up the stairs, the Deputy Administrator following them
rapidly.

"Seat belt," said Gosigo.

Casher found it and snapped it closed.

"Head belt," said Gosigo.

Casher stared at him. He had never heard of a head belt.

"Pull it down from the roof, sir. Put the net under your
chin."

Casher glanced up.

There was a net fitted snug against the roof of the vehicle,
just above his head. He started to pull it down, but it did not

yield. Angrily, he pulled harder, and it moved slowly downward. *By the Bell and Bank, do they want to hang me in this!* he thought to himself as he dragged the net down. There was a strong fibre belt attached to each end of the net, while the net itself was only fifteen to twenty centimeters wide. He ended up in a foolish position, holding the head belt with both hands lest it snap back into the ceiling and not knowing what to do with it. Gosigo leaned over and, half-impatiently, helped him adjust the web under his chin. It pinched for a moment and Casher felt as though his head were being dragged by a heavy weight.

"Don't fight it," said Gosigo. "Relax."

Casher did. His head was lifted several centimeters into a foam pocket, which he had not previously noticed, in the back of the seat. After a second or two, he realized that the position was odd but comfortable.

Gosigo had adjusted his own head belt and had turned on the lights of the vehicle. They blazed so bright that Casher almost thought they might be a laser, capable of charring the inner doors of the big room.

The lights must have keyed the door.

V

Two panels slip open and a wild uproar of wind and vegetation rushed in. It was rough and stormy but far below hurricane velocity.

The machine rolled forward clumsily and was out of the house and on the road very quickly.

The sky was brown, bright luminous brown, shot through with streaks of yellow. Casher had never seen a sky of that color on any other world he had visited, and in his long exile he had seen many planets.

Gosigo, staring straight ahead, was preoccupied with keeping the vehicle right in the middle of the black, soft, tarry road.

"Watch it!" said a voice speaking right into his head.

It was Gosigo, using an intercom which must have been built into the helmets.

Casher watched, though there was nothing to see except for the rush of mad wind. Suddenly the groundcar turned dark, spun upside down, and was violently shaken. An oily, pungent stench of pure fetor immediately drenched the whole car.

Gosigo pulled out a panel with a console of buttons. Light and fire, intolerably bright, burned in on them through the windshield and the portholes on the side.

The battle was over before it began.

The groundcar lay in a sort of swamp. The road was visible thirty or thirty-five meters away.

There was a grinding sound inside the machine and the groundcar righted itself. A singular sucking noise followed, then the grinding sound stopped. Casher could glimpse the big corkscrews on the side of the car eating their way into the ground.

At last the machine was steady, pelted only by branches, leaves, and what seemed like kelp.

A small tornado was passing over them.

Gosigo took time to twist his head sidewise and to talk to Casher.

"An air-whale swallowed us and I had to burn our way out."

"A what?" cried Casher.

"An air-whale," repeated Gosigo calmly on the intercom. "There are no indigenous forms of life on this planet, but the imported Earth forms have changed wildly since we brought them in. The tornadoes lifted the whales around enough so that some of them got adapted to flying. They were the meat-eating kind, so they like to crack our groundcars open and eat the goodies inside. We're safe enough from them for the time being, provided we can make it back to the road. There are a few wild men who live in the wind, but they would not become dangerous to us unless we found ourselves really helpless. Pretty soon I can unscrew us from the ground and try to get back on the road. It's not really too far from here to Ambiloxi."

The trip to the road was a long one, even though they could see the road itself all the time that they tried various approaches.

The first time, the groundcar tipped ominously forward. Red lights showed on the panel and buzzers buzzed. The great spiked wheels spun in vain as they chewed their way into a bottomless quagmire.

Gosigo, calling back to his passenger, cried, "Hold steady! We're going to have to shoot ourselves out of this one backward!"

Casher did not know how he could be any steadier, belted, hooded and strapped as he was, but he clutched the arms of his seat.

The world went red with fire as the front of the car spat flame in rocket-like quantities. The swamp ahead of them boiled into steam, so that they could see nothing. Gosigo changed the windshield from visual to radar, and even with radar there was not much to be seen—nothing but a gray swirl for formless wraiths, and the weird lurching sensation as the machine fought its way back to solid ground. The console suddenly showed green and Gosigo cut the controls. They were back where they had been, with the repulsive burnt entrails of the air-whale scattered among the coral trees.

"Try again," said Gosigo, as though Casher has something to do with the matter.

He fiddled with the controls and the groundcar rose several feet. The spikes on the wheels had been hydraulically extended until they were each at least 150 centimeters long. In sensation, the car felt like a large enclosed bicycle as it teetered on its big wheels. The wind was strong and capricious but there was no tornado in sight.

"Here we go," said Gosigo redundantly. The groundcar pressed forward in a mad rush, hastening obliquely through the vegetation and making for the highway on Casher's right.

A bone-jarring crash told them that they had not made it. For a moment he was too dizzy to see where they were.

He was glad of his helmet and happy about the web brace which held his neck. That crash would have killed him if he had not had full protection.

Gosigo seemed to think the trip normal. His classic Hindu features relaxed in a wise smile as he said, "Hit a boulder. Fell on our side. Try again."

Casher managed to gasp, "Is the machine unbreakable?"

There was a laugh in Gosigo's voice when he answered, "Almost. We're the most vulnerable items in it."

Again fire spat at the ground, this time from the side of the groundcar. It balanced itself precariously on the four high wheels. Gosigo turned on the radar screen to look through the steam which their own jets had called up.

There the road was, plain and near.

"Try again!" he shouted, as the machine lunged forward and then performed a veritable ballet on the surface of the marsh. It rushed, slowed, turned around on a hummock, gave itself an assist with the jets and then scrambled through the water.

Casher saw the inverted cone of a tornado, half a kilometer or less away, veering toward them.

Gosigo sensed his unspoken thought, because he answered, "Problem: who gets to the road first, that or we?"

The machine bucked, lurched, twisted, spun.

Casher could see nothing any more from the windscreen in front, but it was obvious that Gosigo knew what he was doing.

There was the sickening, stomach-wrenching twist of a big drop and then a new sound was heard—a grinding as of knives.

Gosigo, unworried, took his head out of the headnet and looked over at Casher with a smile. "The twister will probably hit us in a minute or two, but it doesn't matter now. We're on the road and I've bolted us to the surface."

"Bolted?" gasped Casher.

"You know, those big screws on the outside of the car. They were made to go right into the road. All the roads here are neo-asphaltum and self-repairing. There will be traces of them here when the last known person on the last known planet is dead. These are *good* roads." He stopped for the sudden hush. "Storm's going over us . . ."

It began again before he could finish his sentence. Wild raving winds tore at the machine which sat so solid that it seemed bedded in permastone.

Gosigo pushed two buttons and then calibrated a dial. He squinted at his instruments and then pressed a button mounted on the edge of his navigator's seat. There was a sharp explosion, like a blasting of rock by chemical methods.

Casher started to speak but Gosigo held out a warning hand for silence.

He tuned his dials quickly. The windscreen faded out, radar came on and then went off, and at last a bright map—bright red in background with sharp gold lines, appeared across the whole width of the screen. There were a dozen or more bright points on the map. Gosigo watched these intently.

The map blurred, faded, dissolved into red chaos.

Gosigo pushed another button and then could see out of the front glass screen again.

"What was that?" asked Casher.

"Miniaturized radar rocket. I sent it up twelve kilometers for a look around. It transmitted a map of what it saw and I put it on our radar screen. The tornadoes are heavier than usual, but I think we can make it. Did you notice the top right of the map?"

"The top right?" asked Casher.

"Yes, the top right. Did you see what was there?"

"Why, nothing," said Casher. "Nothing was there."

"You're utterly right," said Gosigo. "What does that mean to you?"

"I don't understand you," said Casher. "I suppose it means that there is nothing there."

"Right again. But let me tell you something. There never is."

"Never is what?"

"Anything," said Gosigo. "There never is anything on the maps at that point. That's east of Ambiloxi. That's Beauregard. It never shows on the maps. Nothing happens there."

"No bad weather—ever?" asked casher.

"Never," said Gosigo.

"Why not?" asked Casher.

"*She* will not permit it," said Gosigo firmly, as though his words made sense.

"You mean, her weather machines work?" said Casher, grasping for the only rational explanation possible.

"Yes," said Gosigo.

"Why?"

"She pays for them."

"How can she?" exclaimed Casher. "Your whole world of Henriada is bankrupt!"

"Her part isn't."

"Stop mystifying me," said Casher. "Tell me who she is and what this is all about."

"Put your head in the net," said Gosigo. "I'm not making puzzles because I want to do so. I have been commanded not to talk."

"Because you are a forgetty?"

"What's that got to do with it? Don't talk to me that way. Remember, I am not an animal or an underperson. I may be your servant for a few hours, but I am a *man*. You'll find out, soon enough. *Hold tight!*"

The groundcar came to a panic stop, the spiked teeth eating into the resilient firm neo-asphaltum of the road. At the instant they stopped, the outside corkscrews began chewing their way into the ground. First Casher felt as though his eyes were popping out, because of the suddenness of the deceleration; now he felt like holding the arms of his seat as the tornado reached directly for their car, plucking at it again and again. The enormous outside screws held and he could feel the car straining to meet the gigantic suction of the storm.

"Don't worry," shouted Gosigo over the noise of the storm. "I always pin us down a little bit more by firing the quick-rockets straight up. These cars don't often go off the road."

Casher tried to relax.

The funnel of the tornado, which seemed almost like a living being, plucked after them once or twice more and then was gone.

This time, Casher had seen no sign of the air-whales which rode the storms. He had seen nothing but rain and wind and desolation.

The tornado was gone in a moment. Ghostlike shapes trailed after it in enormous prancing leaps.

"Wind-men," said Gosigo glancing at them incuriously. "Wild people who have learned to live on Henriada. They

aren't much more than animals. We are close to the territory
of the lady. They would not dare attack us here."

Casher O'Neill was too stunned to query the man or to
challenge him.

Once more the car picked itself up and coursed along the
smooth, narrow, winding neo-asphaltum road, almost as
though the machine itself were glad to function and to
function well.

VI

Casher could never quite remember when they went from
the howling wildness of Henriada into the stillness and
beauty of the domains of Mister Murray Madigan. He could
recall the feeling but not the facts.

The town of Ambiloxi eluded him completely. It was so
normal a town, so old-fashioned a little town that he could
not think of it very much. Old people sat on the wooden
boardwalk taking their afternoon look at the strangers who
passed through. Horses were tethered in a row along main
street, between the parked machines. It looked like a
peaceful picture from the ancient ages.

Of tornadoes there was no sign, nor of the hurt and ruin
which showed around the house of Rankin Meiklejohn.
There were few underpeople or robots about, unless they
were so cleverly contrived as to look almost exactly like real
people. How can you remember something which is
pleasant and non-memorable? Even the buildings did not
show signs of being fortified against the frightful storms

which had brought the prosperous planet of Henriada to a condition of abandonment and ruin.

Gosigo, who had a remarkable talent for stating the obvious, said tonlessly. "The weather machines are working here. There is no need for special precaution."

But he did not stop in the town for rest, refreshments, conversation or fuel. He went through deftly and quietly, the gigantic armored groundcar looking out of place among the peaceful and defenseless vehicles. He went as though he had been on the same route many times before, and knew the routine well.

Once beyond Ambiloxi he speeded up, though at a moderate pace, compared to the frantic elusive action he had taken against storms in the earlier part of the trip. The landscape was earthlike . . . wet . . . and most of the ground was covered with vegetation.

Old radar countermissile towers stood along the road. Casher could not imagine their possible use, even though he was sure, from the looks of them, that they were long obsolete.

"What's the countermissile radar for?" he asked, speaking comfortably now that his head was out of the head net.

Gosigo turned around and gave him a tortured glance in which pain and bewilderment were mixed. "Countermissile radar? Countermissile radar? I don't know that word, though it seems as though I should . . ."

"Radar is what you were using to see with, back in the storm, when the ceiling and visibility were zero."

Gosigo turned back to his driving, narrowly missing a tree. "That? That's just artificial vision. Why did you use the word 'countermissile radar'? There isn't any of that stuff here except what we have on our machine, though the mistress may be watching us if her set is on."

"Those towers," said Casher. "They look like countermissile towers from the ancient times."

"Towers. There aren't any towers here," snapped Gosigo.

"Look," cried Casher. "Here are two more of them."

"No man made those. They aren't buildings. It's just air coral. Some of the coral which people brought from earth mutated and got so it could live in the air. People used to plant it for windbreaks, before they decided to give up Henriada and move out. They didn't do much good, but they are pretty to look at."

They rode along a few minutes without asking questions. Tall trees had spanish moss trailing over them. They were close to a sea. Small marshes appeared to the right and left of the road; here, where the endless tornadoes were kept out, everything had a park-like effect. The domains of the estate of Beauregard were unlike anything else on Henriada—an area of peaceful wildness in a world which was rushing otherwise toward uninhabitability and ruin. Even Gosigo seemed more relaxed, more cheerful as he steered the groundcar along the pleasant elevated road.

Gosigo sighed, leaned forward, managed the controls and brought the car to a stop.

He turned around calmly and looked full-face at Casher O'Neill.

"You have your knife?"

Casher automatically felt for it. It was there, safe enough in his bootsheath. He simply nodded.

"You have your orders."

"You mean, killing the girl?"

"Yes," said Gosigo, "killing the girl."

"I remember that. You didn't have to stop the car to tell me that."

"I'm telling you now," said Gosigo, his wise Hindu face showing neither humor nor outrage. "Do it."

"You mean, kill her? Right at first sight?"

"Do it," said Gosigo, "you have your orders."

"I'm the judge of that," said Casher. "It will be on my conscience. Are you watching me for the Administrator?"

"That drunken fool?" said Gosigo. "I don't care about him, except that I am a forgetty and I belong to him. We're in *her* territory now. You are going to do whatever she wants. You have orders to kill her. All right. Kill her."

"You mean—she wants to be murdered?"

"Of course not!" said Gosigo, with the irritation of an adult who has to explain too many things to an inquisitive child.

"Then how can I kill her without finding out what this is all about?"

"She knows. She knows herself. She knows her master. She knows this planet. She knows me and she knows something about you. Go ahead and kill her, since those are your orders. If she wants to die, that's not for you or me to decide. It's her business. If she does not want to die, you will not succeed."

"I'd like to see the person," said Casher, "who could stop me in a sudden knife attack. Have *you* told her that I am coming?"

"I've told her nothing, but she knows we are coming and she is pretty sure what you have been sent for. Don't think about it. Just do what you are told. Jump for her with the knife. She will take care of the matter."

"But—" cried Casher.

"Stop asking questions," said Gosigo. "Just follow orders and remember that she will take care of you. Even you." He started up the groundcar.

Within less than a kilometer they had crossed a low ridge of land and there before them lay Beauregard—the mansion at the edge of the waters, its white pillars shining, its pergolas glistening in the bright air, its yards and palmettos tidy.

Casher was a brave man, but he felt the palms of his hands go wet when he realized that in a minute or two he would have to commit a murder.

VII

The groundcar swung up the drive. It stopped. Without a word, Gosigo activated the door. The air smelled calm, sea-wet, salt and yet coolly fresh.

Casher jumped out and ran to the door.

He was surprised to feel that his legs trembled as he ran.

He had killed before, real men in real quarrels. Why should a mere animal matter to him?

The door stopped him.

Without thinking, he tried to wrench it open.

The knob did not yield and there was no automatic control in sight. This was indeed a very antique sort of house. He struck the door with his hands. The thuds sounded around him. He could not tell whether they resounded in the house. No sound or echo came from beyond the door.

He began rehearsing the phrase, "I want to see Mister and Owner Madigan. . . ."

The door did open.

A little girl stood there.

He knew her. He had always known her. She was his sweetheart, come back out of his childhood. She was the sister he had never had. She was his own mother, when young. She was at the marvelous age, somewhere between ten and thirteen, where the child—as the phrase goes—"becomes an old child and not a raw grown-up." She was kind, calm, intelligent, expectant, quiet, inviting, unafraid.

She felt like someone he had never left behind: yet, at the same moment, he knew he had never seen her before.

He heard his voice asking for the Mister and Owner Madigan while he wondered, at the back of his mind, who the girl might be. Madigan's daughter? Neither Rankin Meiklejohn nor the deputy had said anything about a human family.

The child looked at him levelly.

He must have finished braying his question at her.

"Mister and Owner Madigan," said the child, "sees no one this day, buy you are seeing me." She looked at him levelly and calmly. There was an odd hint of humor, of fearlessness, in her stance.

"Who are you?" he blurted out.

"I am the housekeeper of this house."

"You?" he cried, wild alarm beginning in his throat.

"My name," she said, "is T'ruth."

His knife was in his hand before he knew how it had gotten there. He remembered the advice of the Administrator: *plunge, plunge, stab, stab, run!*

She saw the knife but her eyes did not waver from his face.

He looked at her uncertainly.

If this was an underperson, it was the most remarkable one he had ever seen. But even Gosigo had told him to do his duty, to stab, to kill the woman named T'ruth. Here she was. He could not do it.

He spun the knife in the air, caught it by its tip, and held it out to her, handle first.

"I was sent to kill you," he said, "but I find I cannot do it. I have lost a cruiser."

"Kill me if you wish," she said, "because I have no fear of you."

Her calm words were so far outside his experience that he took the knife in his left hand and lifted his arm as if to stab toward her.

He dropped his arm.

"I cannot do it," he whined. "What have you done to me?"

"I have done nothing to you. You do not wish to kill a child and I look to you like a child. Besides, I think you love me. If this is so, it must be very uncomfortable for you."

Casher heard his knife clatter to the floor as he dropped it. He had never dropped it before.

"Who are you," he gasped, "that you should do this to me?"

"I am me," she said, her voice as tranquil and happy as that of any girl, provided that the girl was caught at a moment of great happiness and poise. "I am the housekeeper of this house." She smiled almost impishly and added. "It seems that I must almost be the ruler of this planet as well." Her voice turned serious. *"Man,"* she said, "can't you see it, man? I am an animal, a turtle. I am incapable of disobeying the word of man. When I was little I was trained and I was given orders. I shall carry out those orders as long as I live. When I look at you, I feel strange. You look as though you loved me already, but you do not know what to do. Wait a moment. I must let Gosigo go."

The shining knife on the floor of the doorway, she saw; she stepped over it.

Gosigo had gotten out of the groundcar and was giving her a formal, low bow.

"Tell me," she cried, "what have you just seen!" There was friendliness in her call, as though the routine were an old game.

"I saw Casher O'Neill bound up the steps. You yourself opened the door. He thrust his dagger into your throat and the blood spat out in a big stream, rich and dark and red. You died in the doorway. For some reason Casher O'Neill went on into the house without saying anything to me. I became frightened and I fled."

He did not look frightened at all.

"If I am dead," she said, "how can I be talking to you?"

"Don't ask me," cried Gosigo. "I am just a forgetty. I always go back to the Honorable Rankin Meidlejohn, each time that you are murdered, and I tell him the truth of what I saw. Then he gives me the medicine and I tell him something else. At that point he will get drunk and gloomy again, the way that he always does."

"It's a pity," said the child. "I wish I could help him, but I can't. He won't come to Beauregard."

"Him?" Gosigo laughed. "Oh, no, not him! Never! He just sends other people to kill you."

"And he's never satisfied," said the child sadly, "No matter how many times he kills me!"

"Never," said Gosigo cheerfully, climbing back into the groundcar. "Bye now."

"Wait a moment," she called. "Wouldn't you like something to eat or drink before you drive back? There's a bad clutch of storms on the road."

"Not me," said Gosigo. "He might punish me and make me a forgetty all over again. Say, maybe that's already happened. Maybe I'm a forgetty who's been put through it several times, not just once." Hope surged into his voice. "T'ruth! T'ruth! Can *you* tell me?"

"Suppose I did tell you," said she. "What would happen?"

His face became sad, "I'd have a convulsion and forget what I told you. Well, good-bye anyhow. I'll take a chance on the storms. If you ever see that Casher O'Neill again," called Gosigo, looking right through Casher O'Neill, "tell him I liked him but that we'll never meet again."

"I'll tell him," said the girl gently. She watched as the heavy brown man climbed nimbly into the car. The top crammed shut with no sound. The wheels turned and in a moment the car had disappeared behind the palmettoes in the drive.

While she had talked to Gosigo in her clear warm high girlish voice, Casher had watched her. He could see the thin shape of her shoulders under the light blue shift that she wore. There was the suggestion of a pair of panties under the dress, so light was the material. Her hips had not begun to fill. When he glanced at her in one-quarter profile, he could see that her cheek was smooth, her hair well-combed, her little breasts just beginning to bud on her chest. Who was this child who acted like an empress?

She turned back to him and gave him a warm, apologetic smile.

"Gosigo and I always talk over the story together. Then he goes back and Meiklejohn does not believe it and spends unhappy months planning my murder all over again. I suppose, since I am just an animal, that I should not call it a 'murder' when somebody tries to kill me, but I resist, of course. I do not care about me, but I have orders, strong orders, to keep my master and his house safe from harm."

"How old are you?" asked Casher. He added, "—if you can tell the truth."

"I can tell nothing but the truth. I am conditioned. I am nine hundred and six earth-years old."

"Nine hundred?" he cried. "But you look like a child. . . ."

"I am a child," said the girl, "and not a child. I am an earth turtle, changed into human form by the convenience of man. My life expectancy was increased three hundred times when I was modified. They tell me that my normal life span should have been three hundred years. Now it is ninety thousand years, and sometimes I am afraid. You will be dead of happy old age, Casher O'Neill, while I am still opening the drapes in this house to let the sunlight in. But let's not stand in the door and talk. Come on in and get some refreshments. You're not going anywhere, you know."

Casher followed her into the house but he put his worry into words, "You mean I am your prisoner."

"Not my prisoner, Casher. Yours. How could you cross that ground which you traveled in the groundcar? You could get to the ends of my estate all right, but then the storms would pick you up and whirl you away to a death which nobody would even see."

She turned into a big old room, bright with light-colored wooden furniture.

Casher stood there, awkwardly. He had returned his knife to its bootsheath when they left the vestibule. Now he felt very odd, sitting with his victim on a sun-porch.

T'ruth was untroubled. She rang a brass bell which stood on an old-fashioned round table. Feminine footsteps clattered in the hall. A female servant entered the room, dressed in a black dress with a white apron. Casher had seen such servants in the old drama cubes, but he had never expected to meet one in the flesh.

"We'll have high tea," said T'ruth. "Which do you prefer, tea or coffee, Casher? Or I have beer and wines. Even two bottles of whiskey brought all the way from Earth."

"Coffee would be fine for me," said Casher.

"And you know what I want, Eunice," said T'ruth to the servant.

"Yes, *ma'am*," said the maid, disappearing.

Casher leaned forward.

"That servant—is she human?"

"Certainly," said T'ruth.

"Then why is she working for an underperson like you? I mean—I don't mean to be unpleasant or anything—but I mean—that's against all laws."

"Not here, on Henriada, it isn't."

"And why not?" persisted Casher.

"Because, on Henriada, I am myself the law."

"But the government—?"

"It's gone."

"The Instrumentality?"

T'ruth frowned. She looked like a wise, puzzled child. "Maybe you know that part better than I do. They leave an Administrator here, probably because they do not have any other place to put him and because he needs some kind of work to keep him alive. Yet they do not give him enough real power to arrest my master or to kill me. They ignore me. It seems to me that if I do not challenge them, they leave me alone."

"But their rules—?" insisted Casher.

"They don't enforce them, neither here in Beauregard nor over in the town of Ambiloxi. They leave it up to me to keep these places going. I do the best I can."

"That servant, then? Did they lease her to you?"

"Oh, no," laughed the girl-woman. "She came to kill me twenty years ago, but she was a forgetty and she had no place else to go, so I trained her as a maid. She has a contract with my master, and her wages are paid every month into the satellite above the planet. She can leave if she ever wants to. I don't think she will."

Casher sighed. "This is all too hard to believe. You are a child, but you are almost a thousand years old. You're an underperson, but you command a whole planet—"

"Only when I need to!" she interrupted him.

"You are wiser than most of the people I have ever known and yet you look young. How old do you feel?"

"I feel like a child," she said, "a child one thousand years old. And I have had the education and the memory and the experiance of a wise lady stamped right into my brain."

"Who was the lady?" asked Casher.

"The Owner and Citizen Agatha Madigan. The wife of my master. As she was dying they transcribed her brain on mine. That's why I speak so well and know so much."

"But that's illegal!" cried Casher.

"I suppose it was," said T'ruth, "but my master had it done, anyhow."

Casher leaned forward in his chair. He looked earnestly at the person. One part of him still loved her for the wonderful little girl whom he had thought she was, but another part was in awe of being more powerful than anyone he had seen before. She returned his gaze with that composed half-smile which was wholly feminine and completely self-possessed; she looked tenderly upon him as their faces were reflected by the yellow morning light of Henriada. "I begin to understand," he said, "that you are what you have to be. It is very strange, here in this forgotten world."

"Henriada is strange," she said, "and I suppose that I must seem strange to you. You are right, though, about each of us being what she has to be. Isn't that liberty itself? If we each one *must* be something, isn't liberty the business of finding it out and then doing it—that one job, that uttermost mission compatible with our natures? How terrible it would be, to be something and never know what!"

"Like who?" said Casher.

"Like Gosigo, perhaps. He was a great king and he was a good king, on some faraway world where they still need kings. But he committed an intolerable mistake and the Instrumentality made him into a forgetty and sent him here."

"So that's the mystery!" said Casher. "And what am I?"

She looked at him calmly and steadfastly before she answered. "You are a killer, too. It must make your life very hard in many ways. You keep having to justify yourself."

This was so close to the truth—so close to Casher's long worries as to whether justice might not just be a cover name for "revenge"—that it was his turn to gasp and be silent.

"And I have work for you," added the amazing child.

"Work? Here?"

"Yes. Something much worse than killing. And you must do it, Casher, if you want to go away from here before I die, eighty-nine thousand years from now." She looked around. "Hush!" she added. "Eunice is coming and I do not want to frighten her by letting her know the terrible things that you are going to have to do."

"Here?" he whispered urgently. "Right here, in this house?"

"Right here in this house," she said in a normal voice, as Eunice entered the room bearing a huge tray covered with plates of food and two pots of beverage.

Casher stared at the human woman who worked so cheerfully for an animal; but neither Eunice, who was busy setting things out on the table, nor T'ruth, who, turtle and woman that she was, could not help rearranging the dishes with gentle peremptories, paid the least attention to him.

The words rang in his head. "In this house . . . something worse than killing." They made no sense. Neither did it make sense to have high tea before five hours, decimal time.

He sighed and they both glanced at him, Eunice with amused curiosity, T'ruth with affectionate concern.

"He's taking it better than most of them do, ma'am," said Eunice. "Most of them who come here to kill you are very upset when they find out that they cannot do it."

"He's a killer, Eunice, a real killer, so I think he wasn't too bothered."

Eunice turned to him very pleasantly and said, "A killer, sir. It's a pleasure to have you here. Most of them are terrible amateurs and then the lady has to heal them before we can find something for them to do."

Casher couldn't resist a spot inquiry. "Are all the other would-be killers still here?"

"Most of them, sir. The ones that nothing happened to. Like me. Where else would we go? Back to the Administrator, Rankin Meiklejohn?" She said the last with heavy scorn indeed, curtsied to him, bowed deeply to the woman-girl T'ruth, and left the room.

T'ruth looked friendlily at Casher O'Neill. "I can tell that you will not digest your food if you sit here waiting for bad news. When I said you had to do something worse than killing, I suppose I was speaking from a woman's point of view. We have a homicidal maniac in the house. He is a house guest and he is covered by Old North Australian law. That means we cannot kill him or expel him, though he is almost as immortal as I am. I hope that you and I can frighten him away from molesting my master. I cannot cure him or love him. He is too crazy to be reached through his emotions. Pure, utter awful fright might do it, and it takes a man for that job. If you do this, I will reward you richly."

"And if I don't?" said Casher.

Again she stared at him as though she were trying to see through his eyes all the way down to the bottom of his soul; again he felt for her that tremor of compassion, ever so slightly tinged with male desire, which he had experienced when he first met her in the doorway of Beauregard.

Their locked glances broke apart.

T'ruth looked at the floor. "I cannot lie," she said, as though it were a handicap. "If you do not help me I shall have to do the things which it is in my power to do. The chief thing is nothing. To let you live here, to let you sleep and eat in this house until you get bored and ask me for some kind of routine work around the estate. I could make you work," she went on, looking up at him and blushing all the way to the top of her bodice, "by having you fall in love with me, but that would not be kind. I will not do it that way. Either you make a deal with me or you do not. It's up to you. Anyhow, let's eat first. I've been up since dawn, expecting one more killer. I even wondered if you might be the one who would succeed. That would be terrible, to leave my master all alone!"

"But you—wouldn't you yourself mind being killed?"

"Me? When I've already lived a thousand years and have eighty-nine thousand more to go! It couldn't matter less to me. Have some coffee."

And she poured his coffee.

VIII

Two or three times Casher tried to get the coversation back to the work at hand, but T'ruth diverted him with trivialities. She even made him walk to the enormous window, where they could see far across the marshes and the bay. The sky in the remote distance was dark and full of worms. Those were tornadoes, beyond the reach of her weather machines, which coursed around the rest of Henriada but stopped short at the boundaries of Ambiloxi and Beauregard. She made him admire the weird coral castles which had built themselves up from the bay bottom, hundreds of feet into the air. She tried to make him see a family of wild windpeople who were slyly and gently stealing apples from her orchard, but either his eyes were not used to the landscape or T'ruth could see much further than he could.

This was a world rich in water. If it had not been located within a series of bad pockets of space, the water itself could have become an export. Mankind had done the best it could, raising kelp to provide the iron and phosphorus so often lacking in off-world diets, controlling the weather at great expense. Finally the Instrumentality recommended that they give up. The exports of Henriada never quite

balanced the imports. The subsidies had gone far beyond
the usual times. The earth-life had adapted with a vigor
which was much too great. Ordinary forms rapidly found
new shapes, challenged by the winds, the rains, the novel
chemistry and the odd radiation patterns of Henriada. Killer
whales became airborne, coral took to the air, human babies
lost in the wind sometimes survived to become subhuman
and wild, jellyfish became sky-sweepers. The former
inhabitants of Henriada had chosen a planet at a reasonable
price—not cheap, but reasonable—from the owner who had
in turn bought it from a post-Soviet settling cooperative.
They had leased the new planet, had worked out an ecology,
had emigrated, and were now doing well.

Henriada kept the wild weather, the lost hopes, and the
ruins.

And of these ruins, the greatest was Murray Madigan.

Once a prime landholder and host, a gentleman among
gentlemen, the richest man on the whole world, Madigan
had become old, senile, weak. He faced death or catalepsis.
The death of his wife made him fear his own death and with
his turtle-girl T'ruth, he had chosen catalepsis. Most of the
time he was frozen in a trance, his heartbeat imperceptible,
his metabolism very slow. Then, for a few hours or days, he
was normal. Sometimes the sleeps were for weeks, sometimes for years. The Instrumentality doctors had looked him
over—more out of scientific curiosity than from any judicial
right—and had decided that though this was an odd way to
live, it was a legal one. They went away and left him alone.
He had had the whole personality of his dying wife Agatha
Madigan impressed on the turtle-child, though this was
illegal; the doctor had, quite simply, been bribed.

All this was told by T'ruth to Casher as they ate and
drank their way slowly through an immense repast.

An archaic wood fire roared in a real fireplace.

While she talked, Casher watched the gentle movement

of her shoulderblades when she moved forward, the loose movement of her light dress as she moved, the childish face which was so tender, so appealing and yet so wise.

Knowing as little as he did about the planet of Henriada, Casher tried desperately to fit his own thinking together and to make sense out of the predicament in which he found himself. Even if the girl *were* attractive, this told him nothing of the real challenges which he still faced inside this very house. No longer was his preoccupation with getting the power cruiser his main job on Henriada; no evidence was at hand to show that the drunken, deranged Administrator, Rankin Meiklejohn, would give him anything at all unless he, Casher, killed the girl.

Even that had become a forgotten mission. Despite the fact that he had come to the estate of Beauregard for the purpose of killing her, he was now on a journey without a destination. Years of sad experience had taught him that when a project went completely to pieces, he still had the mission of personal survival, if his life were to mean anything to his home planet, Mizzer, and if his return, in any way or any fashion, could bring real liberty back to the Twelve Niles.

So he looked at the girl with a new kind of unconcern. How could she help his plans? Or hinder them? The promises she made were too vague to be of any real use in the sad complicated world of politics.

He just tried to enjoy her company and the strange place in which he found himself.

The Gulf of Esperanza lay just within his vision. At the far horizon he could see the helpless tornadoes trying to writhe their way past the weather machines which still functioned, at the expense of Beauregard, all along the coast from Ambiloxi to Mottile. He could see the shoreline choked with kelp, which had once been a cash crop and was now a nuisance. Ruined buildings in the distance were probably the leftovers of processing plants; the artificial-looking coral castles obscured his view of them.

And this house—how much sense did this house make?

An undergirl, eerily wise, who herself admitted that she had obtained an unlawful amount of conditioning; a master who was a living corpse; a threat which could not even be mentioned freely within the house; a household which seemed to have displaced the planetary government; a planetary government which the Instrumentality, for unfathomable reasons of its own, had let fall into ruin. Why? Why? And why again?

The turtle girl was looking at him. If he had been an art student, he would have said that she was giving him the tender, feminine and irrecoverably remote smile of a Madonna, but he did not know the motifs of the ancient pictures; he just knew that it was a smile characteristic of T'ruth herself.

"You are wondering . . . ?" she said.

He nodded, suddenly feeling miserable that mere words had come between them.

"You are wondering why the Instrumentality let you come here . . . ?"

He nodded again.

"I don't know either," said she, reaching out and taking his hand. His hand felt and looked like the hairy paw of a giant as she held his right hand with her two pretty, well-kept little-girl hands; but the strength of her eyes and the steadfastness of her voice showed that it was she who was giving the reassurance, not he.

The child was helping *him!*

The idea was outrageous, impossible, true.

It was enough to alarm him, to make him begin to pull his hand again. She clutched him with tender softness, with weak strength, and he could not resist her. Again he had the feeling, which had gripped him so strongly when he first met her at the door of Beauregard and failed to kill her, that he had always known her and had always loved her. (Was there not some planet on which eccentric people believed a weird cult, thinking that human beings were endlessly reborn with fragmentary recollections of their own previous human lives? It was almost like that. Here. Now. He did not know the girl but he had always known her. He did not love the girl and yet he had loved her from the beginning of time.)

Said she, so softly that it was almost a whisper: "Wait. . . . Wait. . . . Your death may come through that door pretty soon and I will tell you how to meet it. But before that, even, I have to show you the most beautiful thing in the world."

Despite her little hand lying tenderly and firmly on his, Casher spoke irritably: "I'm tired of talking riddles here on Henriada. The Administrator gives me the mission of killing you and I fail in it. Then you promise me a battle and give me a good meal instead. Now you talk about the battle and start off with some other irrelevance. You're going to make me angry if you keep on and, and, and"—he stammered at last—"and I get pretty useless if I'm angry. If you want me to do a fight for you, let me know the fight and let me go do it now. I'm willing enough."

Her remote, kind half-smile did not waver. "Casher," she said, "what I am going to show you is your most important weapon in the fight."

With her free left hand she tugged at the fine chain of a thin gold necklace. Some kind of a piece of jewelry came out of the top of her shift dress, where she had kept it hidden. It was the image of two pieces of wood with a man nailed to them.

Casher stared and then he burst into hysterical laughter.

"Now you've done it, ma'am," he cried. "I'm no use to you or to anybody else. I know what that is, and up to now

I've just suspected it. It's what the robot, rat and Copt agreed on when they went exploring back in Space Three. It's the Old Strong Religion. You've put it in my mind and now the next person who meets me will peep it and will wipe it out. Me too, probably, along with it. That's no weapon. That's a defeat. You've done me in. I knew the sign of the Fish a long time ago, but I had a chance of getting away with just that little bit."

"Casher!" she cried. "Casher! Get hold of yourself. You will know nothing about this before you leave Beauregard. You will forget. You will be safe."

He stood on his feet, not knowing whether to run away, to laugh out loud, or to sit down and weep at the silly sad misfortune which had befallen him. To think that he himself had become brain-branded as a fanatic—forever denied travel between the stars—just because an undergirl had shown him an odd piece of jewelry!

"It's not as bad as you think," said the little girl, and stood up too. Her face peered lovingly at Casher's. "Do you think, Casher, that I am afraid?"

"No," he admitted.

"You will not remember this, Casher. Not when you leave. I am not just the turtle-girl T'ruth. I am also the imprint of the citizen Agatha. Have you ever heard of her?"

"Agatha Madigan?" He shook his head slowly. "No. I don't see how . . . No, I'm sure that I never heard of her."

"Didn't you ever hear the story of the Hechizera of Gonfalon?"

Casher looked surprised. "Sure I saw it. It's a play. A drama. It is said to be based on some legend out of immemorial time. The 'space-witch' they called her, and she conjured fleets out of nothing by sheer hypnosis. It's an old story."

"Eleven hundred years isn't so long," said the girl.

"Eleven hundred years, fourteen local months come next tonight."

"You weren't alive eleven hundred years ago," said Casher accusingly.

He stood up from the remains of their meal and wandered over toward the window. That terrible piece of religious jewelry made him uncomfortable. He knew that it was against all laws to ship religion from world to world. What would he do, what could he do, now that he had actually beheld an image of the God Nailed High? That was exactly the kind of contraband which the police and customs robots of hundreds of worlds were looking for.

The Instrumentality was easy about most things, but the transplanting of religion was one of its hostile obsessions. Religions leaked from world to world, anyhow. It was said that sometimes even the underpeople and robots carried bits of religion through space, though this seemed improbable. The Instrumentality left religion alone when it had a settled place on a single planet, but the Lords of the Instrumentality themselves shunned other people's devotional lives and simply took good care that fanaticisms did not once more flare up between the stars, once again bringing wild hope and great death to all the mankinds.

And now, thought Casher, *the Instrumentality has been good to me in its big impersonal collective way, but what will it do when my brain is on fire with forbidden knowledge?*

The girl's voice called him back to himself:

"I have the answer to your problem, Casher," said she, "if you would only listen to me. I *am* the Hechizera of Gonfalon, at least I am as much as any one person can be printed on another."

His jaw dropped as he turned back to her. "You mean that you, child, really are imprinted with this woman Agatha Madigan? Really imprinted?"

"I have all her skills, Casher," said the girl quietly, "and a few more which I have learned on my own."

"But I thought it was just a story. . . ." said Casher. "If you're that terrible woman from Gonfalon, you don't need me. I'm quitting. Now."

Casher walked toward the door. Disgusted, finished, through. She might be a child, she might be charming, she might need help, but if she came from that terrible old story, she did not need him.

"Oh, no, you don't," said she.

IX

Unexpectedly, she took her place in the doorway, barring it.

In her hand was the image of the man on the two pieces of wood.

Ordinarily Casher would not have pushed a lady. Such was his haste that he did so this time. When he touched her, it was like welded steel; neither her gown nor her body yeilded a thousandth of a millimeter to his strong hand and heavy push.

"And now what?" she asked gently.

Looking back, he saw that the real T'ruth, the smiling girl-woman, still stood soft and real in the window.

Deep within, he began to give up; he had heard of hypnotists who could project, but he had never met one as strong as this.

She was doing it. How was she doing it? Or was she

doing it? The operation could be sub-volitional. There might be some art carried over from her animal past which even her re-formed mind could not explain. Operations too subtle, too primordial for analysis. Or skills which she used without understanding.

"I project," she said.

"I see you do," he replied glumly and flatly.

"I do kinesthetics," she said. His knife whipped out of his bootsheath and floated in the air in front of him.

He snatched it out of the air instinctively. It wormed a little in his grasp, but the force on the knife was nothing more than he had felt when passing big magnetic engines.

"I blind," she said. The room went totally dark for him.

"I hear," he said, and prowled at her like a beast, going by his memory of the room and by the very soft sound of her breathing. He had noticed by now that the simulacrum of herself which she had put in the doorway did not make any sound at all, not even that of breathing.

He knew that he was near her. His fingertips reached out for her shoulder or her throat. He did not mean to hurt her, merely to show her that two could play at tricks.

"I stun," she said, and her voice came at him from all directions. It echoed from the ceiling, came from all five walls of the old odd room, from the open windows, from both the doors. He felt as though he were being lifted into space and turned slowly in a condition of weightlessness. He tried to retain self-control, to listen for the one true sound among the many false sounds, to trap the girl by some outside chance.

"I make you remember," said her multiple echoing voice.

For an instant he did not see how this could be a weapon, even if the turtle-girl had learned all the ugly tricks of the Hechizera of Gonfalon.

But then he knew.

He saw his uncle, Kuraf, again. He saw his old apartments vividly around himself. Kuraf was there. The old man was pitiable, hateful, drunk, horrible; the girl on Kuraf's lap laughed at him, Casher O'Neill, and she laughed at Kuraf, too. Casher had once had a teen-ager's passionate concern with sex and at the same time had had a teen-ager's dreadful fear of all the unstated, invisible implications of what the man-woman relationship, gone sour, gone wrong, gone bad, might be. The present-moment Casher remembered the long-ago Casher and as he spun in the web of T'ruth's hypnotic powers he found himself back with the ugliest memory he had.

The killings in the palace at Mizzer.

The colonels had taken Kaheer itself, and they ultimately let Kuraf run away to the pleasure planet of Ttiolle.

But Kuraf's companions, who had debauched the old republic of the Twelve Niles, those people! They did not go. The soldiers, stung to fury, had cut them down with knives. Casher thought of the blood, blood sticky on the floors, blood gushing purple into the carpets, blood bright red and leaping like a fountain when a white throat ended its last gurgle, blood turning brown where handprints, themselves bloody, had left it on marble tables. The warm palace, long ago, had gotten the sweet sick stench of blood all the way through it. The young Casher had never known that people had so much blood inside them, or that so much could pour out on the perfumed sheets, the tables still set with food and drink, or that blood could creep across the floor in growing pools as the bodies of the dead yielded up their last few nasty sounds and their terminal muscular spasms.

Before that day of butchery had ended, one thousand, three hundred and eleven human bodies, ranging in age from two months to eighty-nine years, had been carried out of the palaces once occupied by Kuraf. Kuraf, under sedation, was waiting for a starship to take him to perpetual exile and Casher—Casher himself O'Neill!—was shaking

the hand of Colonel Wedder, whose orders had caused all
the blood. The hand was washed and the nail pared and
cleaned, but the cuff of the sleeve was still rimmed with the
dry blood of some other human being. Colonel Wedder
either did not notice his own cuff, or he did not care.

"Touch and yield!" said the girl-voice out of nowhere.

Casher found himself on all fours in the room, his sight
suddenly back again, the room unchanged, and T'ruth
smiling.

"I fought you," she said.

He nodded. He did not trust himself to speak.

He reached for his water-glass, looking at it closely to see
if there were any blood on it.

Of course not. Not here. Not this time, not this place.

He pulled himself to his feet.

The girl had sense enough not to help him.

She stood there in her thin modest shift, looking very
much like a wise female child, while he stood up and drank
thirstily. He refilled the glass and drank again.

Then, only then, did he turn to her and speak:

"Do you do all that?"

She nodded.

"Alone? Without drugs or machinery?"

She nodded again.

"Child," he cried out, "you are not a person! You're a
whole weapons system all by yourself. What are you,
really? *Who* are you?"

"I am the turtle child T'ruth," she said, "and I am the
loyal property and loving servant of my good master, the
Mister and Owner Murray Madigan."

"Madam," said Casher, "you are almost a thousand
years old. I am at your service. I do hope you will let me go
free later on. And especially, that you will take that
religious picture out of my mind."

As Casher spoke, she picked a locket from the table. He

had not noticed it. It was an ancient watch or a little round box, swinging on a thin gold chain.

"Watch this," said the child, "if you trust me, and repeat what I then say."

(Nothing at all happened: nothing—anywhere.)

Casher said to her, "You're making me dizzy, swinging that ornament. Put it back on. Isn't that the one you were wearing?"

"No, Casher, it isn't."

"What were we talking about?" demanded Casher.

"Something," said she. "Don't you remember?"

"No," said Casher brusquely. "Sorry, but I'm hungry again." He wolfed down a sweet roll encrusted with sugar and decorated with fruits. His mouth full, he washed the food down with water. At last he spoke to her. "Now what?"

She had watched with timeless grace.

"There's no hurry, Casher. Minutes or hours, they don't matter."

"Didn't you want me to fight somebody after Gosigo left me here?"

"That's right," she said, with terrible quiet.

"I seem to have had a fight right here in this room." He stared around stupidly.

She looked around the room, very cool. "It doesn't look as though anybody's been fighting here, does it?"

"There's no blood here, no blood at all. Everything is clean," said he.

"Pretty much so."

"Then why," said Casher, "should I think I had a fight?"

"This wild weather on Henriada sometimes upsets off-worlders until they get used to it," said T'ruth mildly.

"If I didn't have a fight in the past, am I going to get into one in the future?"

The old room with the golden-oak furniture swam around him. The world outside was strange with the sunlit marshes and wide bayous trailing off to the forever-thundering storm, just over the horizon, which lay beyond the weather machines. Casher shrugged and shivered. He looked straight at the girl. She stood erect and looked at him with the even regard of a reigning empress. Her young budding breasts barely showed through the thinness of her shift; she wore golden flat-heeled shoes. Around her neck there was a thin gold chain, but the object on the chain hung down inside her dress. It excited him a little to think of her flat chest barely budding into womanhood. He had never been a man who had an improper taste for children, but there was something about this person which was not childlike at all.

"You are a girl and not a girl. . . ." he said in bewilderment.

She nodded gravely.

"You are that woman in the story, the Hechizera of Gonfalon. You are reborn."

She shook her head, equally seriously. "No, I am not reborn. I am a turtle child, an underperson with very long life, and I have been imprinted with the personality of the Citizen Agatha. This all."

"You stun," he said, "but I do not know how you do it."

"I stun," she said flatly and around the edge of his mind there flickered up hot little torments of memory.

"Now I remember," he cried, "you have me here to kill somebody. You are sending me into a fight."

"You are going to a fight, Casher. I wish I could send somebody else, not you, but you are the only person here strong enough to do the job."

Impulsively he took her hand. The moment he touched her, she ceased to be a child or an underperson. She felt tender and exciting, like the most desirable and important person he had ever known. His sister? But he had no sister. He felt that he was himself terribly, unendurably important to her. He did not want to let her hand go, but she withdrew from his touch with an authority which no decent man could resist.

"You must fight to the death, now, Casher," she said, looking at him as evenly as might a troop commander examining a special soldier selected for a risky mission.

He nodded. He was tired of having his mind confused. He knew something had happened to him after the forgetty, Gosigo, had left him at the front door, but he was not at all sure of what it was. They seem to have had a sort of meal together in this room. He felt himself in love with the child. He knew that she was not even a human being. He remembered something about her living ninety thousand years and he remembered something else about her having gotten the name and the skills of the greatest battle hypnotist of all history, the Hechizera of Gonfalon. There was something strange, something frightening about that chain around her neck: there were things he hoped he would never have to know.

He strained at the thought and it broke like a bubble.

"I'm a fighter," he said. "Give me my fight and let me know."

"He can kill you. I hope not. You must not kill him. He is immortal and insane. But in the law of Old North Australia, from which my master, the Mister and Owner Murray Madigan, is an exile, we must not hurt a house guest, nor may we turn him away in a time of great need."

"What do I *do?*" snapped Casher impatiently.

"You fight him. You frighten him. You make his poor crazy mind fearful that he will meet you again."

"I'm supposed to do this."

"You can," she said very seriously. "I've already tested you. That's where you have the little spot of amnesia about this room."

"But *why?* Why bother? Why not get some of your

human servants and have them tie him up or put him in a padded room?"

"They can't deal with him. He is too strong, too big, too clever, even though insane. Besides, they don't dare follow him."

"Where does he go?" said Casher sharply.

"Into the control room," replied T'ruth, as if it were the saddest phrase ever uttered.

"What's wrong with that? Even a place as fine as Beauregard can't have too much of a control room. Put locks on the control."

"It's not that kind of a control room."

Almost angry, he shouted, "What is it, then?"

"The control room," she answered, "is for a planoform ship. This house. These counties, all the way to Mottile on the one side and to Ambiloxi on the other. The sea itself, way out into the Gulf of Esperanza. All this is one ship."

Casher's professional interest took over. "If it's turned off, he can't do any harm."

"It's not turned off," she said. "My master leaves it on a very little bit. That way, he can keep the weather machines going and make this edge of Henriada a very pleasant place."

"You mean," said Casher, "that you'd risk letting a lunatic fly all these estates off into space."

"He doesn't even fly," said T'ruth gloomily.

"What does he *do*, then?" yelled Casher.

"When he gets at the controls, he just hovers."

"He hovers? By the Bell, girl, don't try to fool me. If you hover a place as big as this, you could wipe out the whole planet any moment. There have been only two or three pilots in the history of space who would be able to hover a machine like this one."

"He can, though," insisted the little girl.

"Who is he, anyhow?"

"I thought you knew. Or had heard somewhere about it. His name is John Joy Tree."

"Tree the Go-Captain?" Casher shivered in the warm room. "He died a long time ago after he made that record flight."

"He did not die. He bought immortality and went mad. He came here and he lives under my master's protection."

"Oh," said Casher. There was nothing else he could say. John Joy Tree, the great Norstrilian who took the first of the Long Plunges outside the galaxy: he was like Magno Taliano of ages ago, who could fly space on his living brain alone.

But fight him? How could anybody fight him?

Pilots are for piloting; killers are for killing; women are for loving or forgetting. When you mix up the purposes, everything goes wrong.

Casher sat down abruptly. "Do you have any more of that coffee?"

"You don't need coffee," she said.

He looked up, inquiringly.

"You're a fighter. You need a war. That's it," she said, pointing with her girlish hand to a small doorway which looked like the entrance to a closet. "Just go in there. He's in there now. Tinkering with the machines again. Making me wait for my master to get blown to bits at any minute! And I've put up with it for over a hundred years."

"Go yourself," he said.

"You've been in a ship's control room," she declared.

"Yes," he nodded.

"You know how people go all naked and frightened inside. You know how much training it takes to make a go-captain. What do you think happens to me?" At last, long last, her voice was shrill, angry, excited, childish.

"What happens?" said Casher dully, not caring very much; he felt weary in every bone. Useless battles, murder he had to try, dead people arguing after their ballads had already grown out of fashion. Why didn't the Hechizera of Gonfalon do her own work?

Catching his thought, she screeched at him, "Because I *can't!*"

"All right," said Casher. "Why not?"

"Because I turn into me."

"You what?" said Casher, a little startled.

"I'm a turtle child. My shape is human. My brain is big. But I'm a *turtle*. No matter how much my master needs me, I'm just a turtle."

"What's that got to do with it?"

"What do turtles do when they're faced with danger? Not underpeople-turtles, but real turtles, little animals. You must have heard of them somewhere."

"I've even seen them," said Casher, "on some world or other. They pull into their shells."

"That's what I do"—she wept—"when I should be defending my master. I can meet most things. I am not a coward. But in that control room, I forget, forget, forget!"

"Send a robot, then!"

She almost screamed at him. "A robot against John Joy Tree? Are you mad, too?"

Casher admitted, in a mumble, that on second thought it wouldn't do much good to send a robot against the greatest go-captain of them all. He concluded, lamely, "I'll go, if you want me to."

"Go now," she shouted, "go right in!"

She pulled at his arm, half-dragging and half-leading him to the little brightened door which looked so innocent.

"But—" he said.

"Keep going," she pleaded. "This is all we ask of you. Don't kill him, but frighten him, fight him, wound him if you must. You can do it. I can't." She sobbed as she tugged at him. "I'd just be *me*."

Before he knew quite what had happened she had opened the door. The light beyond was clear and bright and tinged with blue, the way the skies of Manhome, Mother Earth, were shown in all the viewers.

He let her push him in.

He heard the door click behind him.

Before he even took in the details of the room or noticed the man in the go-captain's chair, the flavor and meaning of the room struck him like a blow against his throat.

This room, he thought, *is hell.*

He wasn't even sure that he remembered where he had learned the word "hell." It denoted all good turned to evil, all hope to anxiety, all wishes to greed.

Somehow, this room was it.

And then. . . .

X

And then the chief occupant of hell turned and looked squarely at him.

If this was John Joy Tree, he did not look insane.

He was a handsome, chubby man with a red complexion, bright eyes, dancing-blue in color, and a mouth which was as mobile as the mouth of a temptress.

"Good day," said John Joy Tree.

"How do you do," said Casher inanely.

"I do not know your name," said the ruddy brisk man, speaking in a tone of voice which was not the least bit insane.

"I am Casher.O'Neill, from the city of Kaheer on the planet Mizzer."

"Mizzer?" John Joy Tree laughed. "I spent a night there, long, long ago. The entertainment was most unusual. But we have other things to talk about. You have come here to kill the undergirl T'ruth. You received your orders from the honorable Rankin Meiklejohn, may he soak in drink! The child has caught you and now she wants you to kill me, but she does not dare utter those words."

John Joy Tree, as he spoke, shifted the spaceship controls to standby, and got ready to get out of his captain's seat.

Casher protested. "She said nothing about killing you. She said you might kill me."

"I might, at that." The immortal pilot stood on the floor. He was a full head shorter than Casher but he was a strong and formidable man. The blue light of the room made him look clear, sharp, distinct.

The whole flavor of the situation tickled the fear-nerves inside Casher's body. He suddenly felt that he wanted very much to go to a bathroom, but he felt—quite surely—that if he turned his back on this man, in this place, he would die like a felled ox in a stockyard. He *had* to face John Joy Tree.

"Go ahead," said the pilot. "Fight me."

"I didn't say that I would fight you," said Casher. "I am supposed to frighten you and I do not know how to do it."

"This isn't getting us anywhere," said John Joy Tree. "Shall we go into the outer room and let poor little T'ruth give us a drink? You can just tell her that you failed."

"I think," said Casher. "that I am more afraid of her than I am of you."

John Joy Tree flung himself into a comfortable passenger's chair. "All right, then. Do something. Do you want to box? Gloves? Bare fists? Or would you like swords? Or wirepoints? There are some over there in the closet. Or we can each take a pilot ship and have a ship-duel out in space."

"That wouldn't make much sense," said Casher, "me

fighting a ship against the greatest go-captain of them all. . . ."

John Joy Tree greeted this with an ugly underlaugh, a barely audible sound which made Casher feel that the whole situation was ridiculous.

"But I do have one advantage," said Casher. "I know who you are and you do not know who I am."

"How could I tell," said John Joy Tree, "when people keep on getting born all over the place?"

He gave Casher a scornful, comfortable grin. There was charm in the man's poise. Keeping his eyes focused directly on Casher, he felt for a carafe and poured himself a drink.

He gave Casher an ironic toast and Casher took it, standing frightened and alone. More alone than he had ever been before in his life.

Suddenly John Joy Tree sprang lightly to his feet and stared with a complete change of expression past Casher. Casher did not dare look around. This was some old fight trick.

Tree spat out the words, *"You've* done it then. This time you will violate all the laws and kill me. This fashionable oaf is not just one more trick."

A voice behind Casher called very softly, "I don't know." It was a man's voice, old, slow and tired.

Casher had heard no one come in.

Casher's years of training stood him in good stead. He skipped sidewise in four or five steps, never taking his eyes off John Joy Tree, until the other man had come into his field of vision.

The man who stood there was tall, thin, yellow-skinned and yellow-haired. His eyes were an old sick blue. He glanced at Casher and said, "I'm Madigan."

Was this the master? thought Casher. *Was this the being whom that lovely child had been imprinted to adore.*

He had no more time for thought.

Madigan whispered, as if to no one in particular, "You find me waking. You find me sane. Watch out."

Madigan lunged for the pilot's controls, but his tall, thin old body could not move very fast.

John Joy Tree jumped out of his chair and ran for the controls, too.

Casher tripped him.

Tree fell, rolled over, and got halfway up, one knee and one foot on the floor. In his hand there shimmered a knife very much like Casher's own.

Casher felt the flame of his body as some unknown force flung him against the wall. He stared, wild with fear.

Madigan had climbed into the pilot's seat and was fiddling with the controls as though he might blow Henriada out of space at any second. John Joy Tree glanced at his old host and then turned his attention to the man in front of him.

There was another man there.

Casher knew him.

He looked familiar.

It was himself, rising and leaping like a snake, left arm weaving the knife for the neck of John Joy Tree.

The image-Casher hit Tree with a thud that resounded through the room.

Tree's bright blue eyes had turned crazy-mad. His knife caught the image-Casher in the abdomen, thrust hard and deep, and left the young man gasping on the floor, trying to push the bleeding entrails back into his belly. The blood poured from the image-Casher all over the rug.

Blood!

Casher suddenly knew what he had to do and how he could do it—all without anybody telling him.

He created a third Casher on the far side of the room and gave him iron gloves. There was himself, unheeded against the wall; there was the dying Casher on the floor; and there was the third, stalking toward John Joy Tree.

"Death is here," screamed the third Casher, with a voice

which Casher recognized as a fierce crazy simulacrum of his own.

Tree whirled around. "You're not real," he said.

Image-Casher stepped around the console and hit Tree with an iron glove. The pilot jumped away, a hand reaching up to his bleeding face.

John Joy Tree screamed at Madigan, who was playing with the dials without even putting on the pinlighter helmet.

"You got her in here," he screamed, "you got her in here with this young man! Get her out!"

"Who?" said Madigan softly and absentmindedly.

"T'ruth. That witch of yours. I claim guest-right by all the ancient laws. *Get her out.*"

The real-Casher, standing at the wall, did not know how he controlled the image-Casher with the iron gloves, but control him he did. He made him speak, in a voice as frantic as Tree's own voice:

"John Joy Tree, I do not bring you death. I bring you blood. My iron hands will pulp your eyes. Blind sockets will stare in your face. My iron hands will split your teeth and break your jaw a thousand times, so that no doctor, no machine will ever fix you. My iron hands will crush your arms, turn your hands into living rags. My iron hands will break your legs. Look at the blood, John Joy Tree. . . . There will be a lot more blood. You have killed me once. See that young man on the floor."

They both glanced at the first image-Casher, who had finally shuddered into death in the great rug. A pool of blood lay in front of the body of the youth.

John Joy Tree turned to the image-Casher and said to him, "You're the Hechizera of Gonfalon. You can't scare me. You're a turtle-girl and can't really hurt me."

"Look at me," said real-Casher.

John Joy Tree glanced back and forth between the duplicates.

Fright began to show.

Both the Cashers now shouted, in crazy voices which came from the depths of Casher's own mind:

"Blood you shall have! Blood and ruin. But we will not kill you. You will live in ruin, blind, emasculated, armless, legless. You will be fed through tubes. You cannot die and you will weep for death but no one will hear you."

"Why?" screamed Tree. "Why? What have I done to you?"

"You remind me," howled Casher, "of my home. You remind me of the blood poured by Colonel Wedder when the poor useless victims of my uncle's lust paid with their blood for his revenge. You remind me of myself, John Joy Tree, and I am going to punish you as I myself might be punished."

Lost in the mists of lunacy, John Joy Tree was still a brave man.

He flung his knife unexpectedly at real-Casher. Image-Casher, in a tremendous bound, leaped across the room and caught the knife on an iron glove. It clattered against the iron glove and then fell silent onto the rug.

Casher saw what he had to see.

He saw the place of Kaheer, covered with death, with the intimate sticky silliness of sudden death—the dead men holding little packages they had tried to save, the girls, with their throats cut, lying in their own blood but with the lipstick still even and the eyebrow-pencil still pretty on their dead faces. He saw a dead child, ripped open from groin upward to chest, holding a broken doll while the child itself, now dead, looked like a broken doll itself. He saw these things and he made John Joy Tree see them, too.

"You're a bad man," said John Joy Tree.

"I am very bad," said Casher.

"Will you let me go, if I never enter this room again?"

Image-Casher snapped off, both the body on the floor and the fighter with the iron gloves. Casher did not know how T'ruth had taught him the lost art of fighter-replication, but he had certainly done it well.

"The lady told me you could go."

"But who are you going to use," said John Joy Tree, calm, sad and logical, "for your dreams of blood if you don't use me?"

"I don't know," said Casher. "I follow my fate. Go now, if you do not want my iron gloves to crush you."

John Joy Tree trotted out of the room, beaten.

Only then did Casher, exhausted, grab a curtain to hold himself upright and look around the room freely.

The evil atmosphere had gone.

Madigan, old though he was, had locked all the controls on standby.

He walked over to Casher and spoke. "Thank you. She did not invent you. She found you and put you to my service."

Casher coughed out, "The girl. Yes."

"*My* girl," corrected Madigan.

"Your girl," said Casher, remembering the sight of that slight feminine body, those budding breasts, the sensitive lips, the tender eyes.

"She could not have thought you up. She is my dead wife over again. The citizeness Agatha might have done it. But not T'ruth."

Casher looked at the man as he talked. The host wore the bottoms of some very cheap yellow pajamas and a washable bathrobe which had one been stripes of purple, lavender and white. Now it was faded, like its wearer. Casher also saw the white clean plastic surgical implants on the man's arms, where the machines and tubes hooked in to keep him alive.

"I sleep a lot," said Murray Madigan, "but I am still the master of Beauregard. I am grateful to you."

The hand was frail, withered, dry, without strength.

The old voice whispered: "Tell her to reward you. You can have anything on my estate. Or you can have anything on Henriada. She manages it all for me." Then the old blue eyes opened wide and sharp and Murray Madigan was once again the man, just momentarily, that he had been hundreds of years ago—a Norstrilian trader, sharp, shrewd, wise and not unkind. He added sharply: "Enjoy her company. She is a good child. But do not take her. Do not try to take her."

"Why not?" said Casher, surprised at his own bluntness.

"Because if you do, she will die. She is *mine*. Imprinted to me. I had her made and she is mine. Without me she would die in a few days. Do not take her."

Casher saw the old man leave the room by a secret door. He left himself, the way he had come in. He did not see Madigan again for two days, and by that time the old man had gone far back into his cataleptic sleep.

XI

Two days later T'ruth took Casher to visit the sleeping Madigan.

"You can't go in there," said Eunice in a shocked voice. "*Nobody* goes in there. That's the master's room."

"I'm taking him in," said T'ruth calmly.

She had pulled a cloth-of-gold curtain aside and she was spinning the combination locks on a massive steel door. It was set in Daimoni material.

The maid went on protesting, "But even you, little ma'am, can't take him in there!"

"Who says I can't?" said T'ruth calmly and challengingly.

The awfulness of the situation sank in on Eunice.

In a small voice she muttered, "If you're taking him in, you're taking him in. But it's never been done before."

"Of course it hasn't, Eunice, not in your time. But Casher O'Neill has already met the mister and owner. He has fought for the mister and owner. Do you think I would take a stray or random guest in to look at the master, just like that?"

"Oh, not at all, no," said Eunice.

"Then go away, woman," said the lady-child. "You don't want to see this door open, do you?"

"Oh, no," shrieked Eunice and fled, putting her hands over her ears as though that would shut out the sight of the door.

When the maid had disappeared. T'ruth pulled with her whole weight against the handle of the heavy door. Casher expected the mustiness of the tomb or the medicinality of a hospital; he was astonished when fresh air and warm sunlight poured out from that heavy, mysterious door. The actual opening was so narrow, so low, that Casher had to step sidewise as he followed T'ruth into the room.

The master's room was enormous. The windows were flooded with perpetual sunlight. The landscape outside must have been the way Henriada looked in its prime, when Mottile was a resort for the carefree millions of vacationers, and Ambiloxi, a port feeding worlds halfway across the galaxy. There was no sign of the ugly snaky storms which worried and pestered Henriada in these later years. Everything was landscape, order, neatness, the triumph of man, as though Poussin had painted it.

The room itself, like the other great living-rooms of the estate of Beauregard, was exuberant neo-baroque in which the architect, himself half-mad, had been given wild license to work out his fantasies in steel, plastic, plaster, wood and stone. The ceiling was not flat, but vaulted. The four corners of the room were each alcoves, cutting deep into the four sides, so that the room was, in effect, an octagon. The propriety and prettiness of the room had been a little diminished by the shoving of the furniture to one side, sofas, upholstered armchairs, marble tables and knickknack stands all in an indescribable melange to the left; while the right hand part of the room—facing the master window with the illusory landscape—was equipped like a surgery with an operating table, hydraulic lifts, bottles of clear and colored fluid hanging from chrome stands and two large devices which (Casher later surmised) must have been heart-lung and kidney machines. The alcoves, in their turn, were wilder. One was an archaic funeral parlor with an immense coffin, draped in black velvet, resting on a heavy teak stand. The next was a spaceship control cabin of the old kind, with the levers, switches and controls all in plain sight—the meters actually read the galactically-stable location of this very place, and to do so they had to whirl mightily—as well as a pilot's chair with the usual choice of helmets and the straps and shock absorbers. The third alcove was a simple bedroom done in very old-fashioned taste, the walls, a Wedgwood blue with deep wine-colored drapes, coverlets and pillowcases marking a sharp but tolerable contrast. The fourth alcove was the copy of a fortress: it might even be a fortress: the door was heavy and the walls looked as though they might be Daimoni material, indestructible by any imaginable means. Cases of emergency food and water were stacked against the walls. Weapons which looked oiled and primed stood in their racks, together with three different calibers of wire-point, each with its own fresh-looking battery.

The alcoves had no people in them.

The parlor was deserted.

The mister and owner Murray Madigan lay naked on the operating table. Two or three wires led to gauges attached to his body. Casher thought that he could see a faint motion of the chest, as the cataleptic man breathed at a rate one-tenth normal or less.

The girl-lady, T'ruth, was not the least embarrassed.

"I check him four or five times a day. I never let people in here. But you're special, Casher. He's talked with you and fought beside you and he knows that he owes you his life. You're the first human person ever to get into this room."

"I'll wager," said Casher, "that the Administrator of Henriada, the Honorable Rankin Meiklejohn, would give up some of his 'honorable' just to get in here and have one look around. He wonders what Madigan is doing when Madigan is doing nothing. . . ."

"He's not just doing nothing," said T'ruth sharply. "He's sleeping. It's not everybody who can sleep for forty or fifty or sixty thousand years and can wake up a few times a month, just to see how things are going."

Casher started to whistle and then stopped himself, as though he feared to waken the unconscious, naked old man on the table. "So that's why he chose *you.*"

T'ruth corrected him as she washed her hands vigorously in a washbasin. "That's why he had me made. Turtle stock, three hundred years. Multiply that with intensive stroon treatments, three hundred times. Ninety thousand years. Then he had me printed to love him and adore him. He's not my master, you know. He's my god."

"Your what?"

"You heard me. Don't get upset. I'm not going to give you any illegal memories. I worship him. That's what I was printed for, when my little turtle eyes opened and they put me back in the tank to enlarge my brain and to make a woman out of me. That's why they printed every memory of the citizeness Agatha Madigan right into my brain. I'm what he wanted. Just what he wanted. I'm the most wanted being on any planet. No wife, no sweetheart, no mother has ever been wanted as much as he wants me now, when he wakes up and knows that I am still here. You're a smart man. Would you trust any machine—any machine at all— for ninety thousand years?"

"It would be hard," said Casher, "to get batteries of monitors long enough for them to repair each other over that long a time. But that means you have ninety thousand years of it. Four times, five times a day. I can't even multiply the numbers. Don't you ever get tired of it?"

"He's my love, he's my joy, he's my darling little boy," she caroled, as she lifted his eyelids and put colorless drops in each eye. Absentmindedly, she explained. "With this slow metabolism, there's always some danger that his eyelids will stick to his eyeballs. This is part of the check-up."

She tilted the sleeping man's head, looked earnestly into each eye. She then stepped a few paces aside and put her face close to the dial of a gently-humming machine. There was the sound of a shot. Casher almost reached for his gun, which he did not have.

The child turned back to him with a free mischievous smile. "Sorry, I should have warned you. That's my noisemaker. I watch the encephalograph to make sure his brain keeps a little auditory intake. It showed up with the noise. He's asleep, very deeply asleep, but he's not drifting downward into death."

Back at the table she pushed Madigan's chin upward so that the head leaned far back on its neck. Deftly holding the forehead, she took a retractor, opened his mouth with her fingers, depressed the tongue and looked down into the throat.

"No accumulation there," she muttered, as if to herself.

She pushed the head back into a comfortable position. She seemed on the edge of another set of operations when it was obvious that an idea occurred to her. "Go wash your hands, thoroughly, over there, at the basin. Then push the timer down and be sure you hold your hands under the sterilizer until the timer goes off. You can help me turn him over. I don't have help here. You're the first visitor."

Casher obeyed and while he washed his hands, he saw the girl drench her hands with some flower-scented unguent. She began to massage the unconscious body with professional expertness, even with a degree of roughness. As he stood with his hands under the sterilizer-drier, Casher marveled at the strength of those girlish arms and those little hands. Indefatigably they stroked, rubbed, pummelled, pulled, stretched and poked the old body. The sleeping man seemed to be utterly unaware of it, but Casher thought that he could see a better skin color and muscle tone appearing.

He walked back to the tasble and stood facing T'ruth.

A huge peacock walked across the imaginary lawn outside the window, his tail shimmering in a paroxysm of colors.

T'ruth saw the direction of Casher's glance.

"Oh, I program that, too. He likes it when he wakes up. Don't you think he was clever, before he went into catalepsis—to have me made, to have me created to love him and to care for him? It helps that I'm a girl. I can't ever love anybody but him, and it's easy for me to remember that this is the man I love. And it's safer for him. Any man might get bored with these responsibilities. I don't."

"Yet—" said Casher.

"Shh," she said, "wait a bit. This takes care." Her strong little fingers were now plowing deep into the abdomen of the naked old man. She closed her eyes so that she could concentrate all her senses on the one act of tactile impression. She took her hands away and stood erect. "All clear," she said. "I've got to find out what's going on inside him. But I don't dare use X-rays on him. Think of the radiation he'd build up in a hundred years or so. He defecates about twice a month while he's sleeping. I've got to be ready for that. I also have to prime his bladder every week or so. Otherwise he would poison himself just with his own body wastes. Here, now, you can help me turn him over. But watch the wires. Those are the monitor controls. They report his physiological process, radio a message to me if anything goes wrong, and meanwhile supply the missing neurophysical impulses if any part of the automatic nervous system began to fade out or just simply went off."

"Has that ever happened?"

"Never," she said, "not yet. But I'm ready. Watch that wire. You're turning him too fast. There now, that's right. You can stand back while I massage him on the back."

She went back to her job of being a masseuse. Starting at the muscles joining the skull to the neck, she worked her way down the body, pouring ointment on her hands from time to time. When she got to his legs, she seemed to work particularly hard. She lifted the feet, bent the knees, slapped the calves.

Then she put on a rubber glove, dipped her hand into another jar—one which opened automatically as her hand approached—and came out with her hand greasy. She thrust her fingers into his rectum, probing, thrusting, groping, her brow furrowed.

Her face cleared as she dropped the rubber glove in a disposal can and wiped the sleeping man with a soft linen towel, which also went into a disposal can. "He's all right. He'll get along well for the next two hours. I'll have to give him a little sugar then. All he's getting now is normal saline."

She stood facing him. There was a faint glow in her cheeks from the violent exercise in which she had been indulging, but she still looked both the child and the lady—the child irrecoverably remote, hidden in her own wisdom from the muddled world of adults, and the lady, mistress in her own home, her own estates, her own planet, serving her master with almost-immortal love and zeal.

"I was going to ask you, back there—" said Casher and then stopped.

"You were going to ask me?"

He spoke heavily. "I was going to ask you, what happens to you when he dies? Either at the right time or possibly before his time. What happens to *you?*"

"I couldn't care less," her voice sang out. He could see by the open, honest smile on her face that she meant it. "I'm *his*. I belong to *him*. That's what I'm *for*. They may have programmed something into me, in case he dies. Or they may have forgotten. What matters is his life, not mine. He's going to get every possible hour of life that I can help him get. Don't you think I'm doing a good job?"

"A good job, yes," said Casher. "A strange one, too."

"We can go now," she said.

"What are those alcoves for?"

"Oh, those—they're his make-believes. He picks one of them to go to sleep in—his coffin, his fort, his ship or his bedroom. It doesn't matter which. I always get him up with the hoist and put him back on his table, where the machines and I can take proper care of him. He doesn't really mind waking up on the table. He has usually forgotten which room he went to sleep in. We can go now."

They walked toward the door.

Suddenly she stopped. "I forgot something. I never forget things, but this is the first time I ever let anybody come in here with me. You were such a *good* friend to him. He'll talk about you for thousands of years. Long, long after you're dead," she added somewhat unnecessarily. Casher looked at her sharply to see if she might be mocking or deprecating him. There was nothing but the little-girl solemnity, the womanly devotion to an established domestic routine.

"Turn your back," she commanded peremptorily.

"Why?" he asked. "Why—when you have trusted me with all the other secrets."

"He wouldn't want you to see this."

"See what?"

"What I'm going to do. When I was the citizeness Agatha—or when I seemed to be her—I found that men are awfully fussy about some things. This is one of them."

Casher obeyed and stood facing the door.

A different odor filled the room—a strong wild scent, like a geranium pomade. He could hear T'ruth breathing heavily as she worked beside the sleeping man.

She called to him: "You can turn around now."

She was putting away a tube of ointment, standing high to get it into its exact position on a tile shelf.

Casher looked quickly at the body of Madigan. It was still asleep, still breathing very lightly and very slowly.

"What on earth did you *do?*"

T'ruth stopped in mid-step: "You're going to get nosy."

Casher stammered mere sounds.

"You can't help it," she said. "People are inquisitive."

"I suppose they are," he said, flushing at the accusation.

"I gave him his bit of fun. He never remembers it when he wakes up, but the cardiograph sometimes shows increased activity. Nothing happened this time. That was my own idea. I read books and decided that it would be good for his body tone. Sometimes he sleeps through a whole earth-year, but usually he wakes up several times a month."

She passed Casher, almost pulled herself clear of the floor tugging on the great inside levers of the main door.

She gestured him past. He stooped and stepped through.

"Turn away again," she said. "All I'm going to do is to spin the dials, but they're cued to give any viewer a bad headache so he will forget the combination. Even robots. I'm the only person tuned to these doors."

He heard the dials spinning but did not look around.

She murmured, almost under her breath, "I'm the only one. The only one."

"The only one for what?" asked Casher.

"To love my master, to care for him, to support his planet, to guard his weather. But isn't he beautiful? Isn't he wise? Doesn't his smile win your heart?"

Casher thought of the fated old wreck of a man with the yellow pajama bottoms. Tactfully, he said nothing.

T'ruth babbled on, quite cheerfully, "He is my father, my husband, my baby son, my master, my owner. Think of that, Casher, he owns me! Isn't he lucky—to have me? And aren't I lucky—to belong to him?"

"But what for?" asked Casher, a little crossly, thinking that he was falling in and out of love with this remarkable girl himself.

"For life!" she cried. "In any form, in any way. I am made for ninety thousand years and he will sleep and wake and dream and sleep again, a large part of that."

"What's the use of it?" insisted Casher.

"The use," she said, "the use? What's the use of the little turtle-egg they took and modified in its memory chains, right down to the molecular level? What's the use of turning me into an undergirl, so that even you have to love me off and on? What's the use of little me, meeting my master for the first time, when I had been manufactured to love him? I can tell you, man, what the use is. Love."

"What did you say?" said Casher.

"I said the use was love. Love is the only end of things. Love on the one side, and death on the other. If you are strong enough to use a real weapon, I can give you a weapon which will put all Mizzer at your mercy. Your cruiser and your laser would just be toys against the weapon of love. You can't fight love. You can't fight me."

They had proceeded down a corridor, forgotten pictures hanging on the walls, unremembered luxuries left untouched by centuries of neglect.

The bright yellow light of Henriada poured in through an open doorway of neglect.

From the room came snatches of a man singing while playing a stringed instrument. Later, Casher found that this was a verse of the Henriada Song, the one which went:

> Don't put your ship in the Boom Lagoon,
> Look up North for the raving wave.
> Henriada's boiled away
> But Ambiloxi's a saving grave.

They entered the room.

A gentleman stood up to greet them.

It was the great go-pilot, John Joy Tree. His ruddy face smiled, his bright blue eyes lit up, a little condescendingly, as he greeted his small hostess, but then his glance took in Casher O'Neill.

The effect was sudden, and evil.

John Joy Tree looked away from both of them. The phrase which he had started to use stuck in his throat.

He said, in a different voice, very "away" and deeply troubled, "There is blood all over this place. There is a man of blood right here. Excuse me. I am going to be sick."

He trotted past them and out the door which they had entered.

"You have passed a test," said T'ruth. "Your help to my master has solved the problem of the captain and honorable John Joy Tree. He will not go near that control room if he thinks that you are there."

"Do you have more tests for me? Still more? By now, you ought to know me well enough not to need tests."

"I am not a person," she said, "but just a built-up copy of one. I am getting ready to give you your weapon. This is a communications room as well as a music room. Would you like something to eat or drink?"

"Just water," he said.

"At your hand," said T'ruth.

A rock-crystal carafe had been standing on the table beside him, unnoticed. Or had she transported it into the room with one of the tricks of the Hechizera, the dreaded Agatha herself? It didn't matter. He drank. Trouble was coming.

XII

T'ruth had swung open a polished cabinet panel. The communicator was the kind they mount in planoforming ships right beside the pilot. The rental on one of them was enough to make any planetary government reconsider its annual budget.

"That's *yours?*" cried Casher.

"Why not?" said the little-girl lady. "I have four or five of them."

"But you're *rich!*"

"I'm not. My master is. I belong to my master, too."

"But things like this. He can't handle them. How does he manage?"

"You mean money and things?" The girlish part of her came out. She looked pleased, happy and mischievous. "I manage them for him. He was the richest man on Henriada when I came here. He had credits of stroon. Now he is about forty times richer."

"He's a Rod McBan!" exclaimed Casher.

"Not even near. Mister McBan had a lot more money than we. But he's rich. Where do you think all the people from Henriada went?"

"I don't know," said Casher.

"To four new planets. They belong to my master and he charges the new settlers a very small land-rent."

"You bought them?" Casher asked.

"For him." T'ruth smiled. "Haven't you heard of planet-brokers?"

"But that's a gambler's business—!" said Casher.

"I gambled," she said, "and I won. Now keep quiet and watch me."

She pressed a button. "Instant message."

"Instant message," repeated the machine. "What priority?"

"War news, double A one, subspace penalty."

"Confirmed," said the machine.

"The planet Mizzer. Now. War and peace information. Will fighting end soon?"

The machine clucked to itself.

Casher, knowing the prices of this kind of communication, almost felt that he could see the arterial spurt of money go out of Henriada's budget as the machines reached across the galaxy, found Mizzer, and came back with the answer.

"Skirmishing. Seventh Nile. Ends three local days."

"Close message," said T'ruth.

The machine went off.

T'ruth turned to him. "You're going home, soon, Casher, if you can pass a few little tests."

He stared at her.

He blurted, "I need my weapons, my cruiser and my laser."

"You'll have weapons. Better ones than those. Right now, I want you to go to the front door. When you have opened the door, you will not let anybody in. Close the door. Then please come back to me here, dear Casher, and if you are still alive, I will have some other things for you to do."

Casher turned in bewilderment. It did not occur to him to contradict her. He could end up a forgetty, like the maidservant Eunice or the Administrator's brown man, Gosigo.

Down the halls, he walked. He met no one except for a few shy cleaning-robots, who bowed their heads politely as he passed.

He found the front door. It stopped him. It looked like wood on the outside, but it was actually a Daimoni door, made of near-indestructible material. There was no sign of a key or dials or controls. Acting like a man in a dream, he took a chance that the door might be keyed to himself. He put his right palm firmly against it, at the left or opening edge.

The door swung in.

Meiklejohn was there. Gosigo held the Administrator upright. It must have been a rough trip. The Administrator's face was bruised and blood trickled from the corner of his mouth. His eyes focused on Casher.

"You're alive. She caught you, too?"

Quite formally, Casher asked, "What do you want in this house?"

"I have come," said the Administrator, "to see her."

"To see whom?" insisted Casher.

The Administrator hung almost slack in Gosigo's arms. By his own standard and in his own way, he was a very brave man, indeed. His eyes looked clear, even though his body was collapsing.

"To see T'ruth, if she will see me," said Rankin Meiklejohn.

"She cannot," said Casher, "see you now. Gosigo!"

The forgetty turned to Casher and gave him a bow.

"You will forget me. You have not seen me."

"I have not seen you, lord. Give my greetings to your lady. Anything else?"

"Yes. Take your master home, as safely and swiftly as you can."

"My lord!" cried Gosigo, though this was an improper title for Casher. Casher turned around.

"My lord, tell her to extend the weather machines for just a few more kilometers and I will have him home safe in ten minutes. At top speed."

"I can tell her," said Casher, "but I cannot promise she will do it."

"Of course," said Gosigo. He picked up the Administrator and began putting him into the groundcar. Rankin Meiklejohn bawled once, like a man crying in pain. It sounded like a blurred version of the name *Murray Madigan*. No one heard it but Gosigo and Casher; Gosigo busy closing the groundcar, Casher pushing on the big house door.

The door clicked.

There was silence.

The opening of the door was remembered only by the warm sweet salty stink of seaweed, which had disturbed the odor-pattern of the changeless, musty old house.

Casher hurried back with the message about the weather machines.

T'ruth received the message gravely. Without looking at the console, she reached out and controlled it with her extended right hand, not taking her eyes off Casher for a moment. The machine clicked its agreement. T'ruth exhaled.

"Thank you, Casher. Now the Instrumentality and the forgetty are gone."

She stared at him, almost sadly and inquiringly. He wanted to pick her up, to crush her to his chest, to rain his kisses on her face. But he stood stock still. He did not move. This was not just the forever-loving turtle-child; this was the real mistress of Henriada. This was the Hechizera of Gonfalon, whom he had formerly thought about only in terms of a wild, melodic grand opera.

"I think you are seeing me, Casher. It is hard to see people, even when you look at them every day. I think I can see you, too, Casher. It is almost time for us both to do the things we have to do."

"Which *we* have to do?" he whispered, hoping she might say something else.

"For me, my work here on Henriada. For you, your fate on your homeland of Mizzer. That's what life is, isn't it? Doing what you have to do in the first place. We're lucky people if we find it out. You are ready, Casher. I am about to give you weapons which will make bombs and cruisers and lasers and bombs seem like nothing at all."

"By the Bell, girl! Can't you tell me what those weapons are?"

T'ruth stood in her innocently revealing sheath, the yellow light of the old music room pouring like a halo around her.

"Yes," she said, "I can tell you now. Me."

"You?"

Casher felt a wild surge of erotic attraction for the innocently voluptuous child. He remembered his first insane impulse to crush her with kisses, to sweep her up with hugs, to exhaust her with all the excitement which his masculinity could bring to both of them.

He stared at her.

She stood there, calm.

That sort of an idea did not ring right.

He was going to get her, but he was going to get something far from fun or folly—something, indeed, which he might not even like.

When at last he spoke, it was out of deep bewilderment of his own thoughts, "What do you mean, you're going to give me yourself? It doesn't sound very romantic to me, nor the tone in which you said it."

The child stepped close to him, reaching up and patting his forehead.

"You're not going to get me for a night's romance, and if you did, you would be sorry. I am the property of my master and of no other man. But I can do something with you which I have never done to anyone else. I can get myself imprinted on you. The technicians are already coming. You will be the turtle child. You will be the citizeness of Agatha Madigan, the Hechizera of Gonfalon herself. You will be many other people. And yourself. You will then win. Accidents may kill you, Casher, but no one will be able to kill you on purpose. Not when you're me. Poor man! Do you know what you will be giving up?"

"What?" he croaked, at the edge of a great fright. He had seen danger before, but never before had danger loomed up from within himself.

"You will not fear death, ever again, Casher. You will have to lead your life minute by minute, second by second, and you will not have the alibi that you are going to die anyhow. You will know that's not special."

He nodded, understanding her words and scrabbling around his mind for a meaning.

"I'm a girl, Casher. . . ."

He looked at her and his eyes widened. She was a girl—a beautiful, wonderful girl. But she was something more. She was the mistress of Henriada. She was the first of the underpeople really and truly to surpass humanity. To think that he had wanted to grab her poor little body. The body—ah, that was sweet!—but the power within it was the kind of thing that empires and religions are made of.

". . . and if you take the print of me, Casher, you will never lie with a woman without realizing that you know more about her than she does. You will be a seeing man among blind multitudes, a hearing person in the world of the deaf. I don't know how much fun romantic love is going to be to you after this."

Gloomily he said, "If I can free my home planet of Mizzer, it will be worth it. Whatever it is."

"You're not going to turn into a woman!" She laughed. "Nothing that easy. But you are going to get wisdom. And I will tell you the whole story of the Sign of the Fish before you leave here."

"Not that, please," he begged. "That's a religion and the Instrumentality would never let me travel again."

"I'm going to have you scrambled, Casher, so that nobody can read you for a year or two. And the Instrumentality is not going to send you back. *I am*. Through space-three."

"It'll cost you a fine, big ship to do it."

"My master will approve when I tell him, Casher. Now give me that kiss you have been wanting to give me. Perhaps you will remember something of it when you come out of scramble."

She stood there. He did nothing.

"Kiss me!" she commanded.

He put his arm around her. She felt like a big little girl. She lifted her face. She thrust her lips up toward his. She stood on tiptoe.

He kissed her the way a man might kiss a picture or a religious object. The heat and fierceness had gone out of his hopes. He had not kissed a girl, but power—tremendous power and wisdom put into a single slight form.

"Is that the way your master kisses you?"

She gave him a quick smile. "How clever of you! Yes, sometimes. Come along now. We have to shoot some children before the technicians are ready. It will give you a good last chance of seeing what you can do, when you have become what I am. Come along, the guns are in the hall."

XIII

They went down an enormous light-oak staircase to a floor which Casher had never seen before. It must have been the entertainment and hospitality of Beauregard long ago, when the mister and owner Murray Madigan was himself young.

The robots did a good job of keeping away the dust and the mildew. Casher saw inconspicuous little air-driers placed at strategic places, so that the rich tooled leather on the walls would not spoil, so that the velvet bar-stools would not become slimy with mold, so that the pool tables would not warp nor the golf clubs go out of shape with age and damp. *By the Bell*, he thought, *that man Madigan could have entertained a thousand people at one time in a place this size.*

The gun-cabinet, now, that was functional. The glass shone. The velvet of oil showed on the steel and walnut of the guns. They were old earth models, very rare and very special. For actual fighting, people used the cheap artillery of the present time or wirepoints for close work. Only the richest and rarest of connoisseurs had the old earth weapons or could use them.

T'ruth touched the guard-robot and waked him. The robot saluted, looked at her face and without further inquiry, opened the cabinet.

"Do you know guns?" said T'ruth to Casher.

"Wirepoints," he said. "Never touched a gun in my life."

118

"Do you mind using a learning-helmet, then? I could teach you hypnotically with the special rules of the Hechizera, but they might give you a headache or upset you emotionally. The helmet is neuro-electric and it has filters."

Casher nodded and saw his reflection nodding in the polished glass doors of the gun-cabinet. He was surprised to see how helpless and lugubrious he looked.

But it was true. Never before in his life had he felt that a situation swept over him, washed him along like a great wave, left him with no choice and no responsibility. Things were her choice now, not his, and yet he felt that her power was benign, self-limited, restricted by factors at which he could no more than guess. He had come for one weapon—the cruiser which he had hoped to get from the Administrator Rankin Meiklejohn. She was offering him something else—psychological weapons in which he had neither experience nor confidence.

She watched him attentively for a long moment and then turned to the gun-watching robot.

"You're little Harry Hadrian, aren't you? The gun-watcher."

"Yes, ma'am," said the silver robot brightly, "and I'm owl-brained too. That makes me very bright."

"Watch this," she said, extending her arms the width of the gun cabinet and then dropping them after a queer flutter of her hands. "Do you know what that means?"

"Yes, ma'am," said the little robot quickly, the emotion showing in his toneless voice by the speed with which he spoke, not by the intonation, "it-means-you-have-taken-over-and-I-am-off-duty! Can-I-go-sit-in-the-garden-and-look-at-the-live-things?"

"Not quite yet, little Harry Hadrian. There are some wind-people out there now and they might hurt you. I have another errand for you first. Do you remember where the teaching helmets are?"

"Silver hats on the third floor in an open closet with a wire running to each hat. Yes."

"Bring one of those as fast as you can. Pull it loose very carefully from its electrical connection."

The little robot disappeared in a sudden, fast, gentle clatter up the stairs.

T'ruth turned back to Casher. "I have decided what to do with you. I am helping you. You don't have to look so gloomy about it."

"I'm not gloomy. The Administrator sent me here on a crazy errand, killing an unknown underperson. I find out that the person is really a little girl. Then I find out that she is not an underperson, but a frightening old dead woman, still walking around alive. My life gets turned upside down. All my plans are set aside. You propose to send me home to fulfill my life's work on Mizzer. I've struggled for this, so many years! Now you're making it all come through, even though you are going to cook me through space-three to do it, and throw in a lot of illegal religion and hypnotic tricks, that I'm not sure I can handle. Now you tell me to come along—to shoot children with guns. I've never done anything like that in my life and yet I find myself obeying you. I'm tired out, girl, tired out. If you have put me in your power, I don't even know it. I don't even want to know it."

"Here you are, Casher, on the ruined wet world of Henriada. In less than a week you will be recovering among the military casualties of Colonel Wedder's army. You will be under the clear sky of Mizzer, and the Seventh Nile will be near you, and you will be ready at long last to do what you have to do. You will have bits and pieces of memories of me—not enough to make you find your way back here or to tell people all the secrets of Beauregard, but enough for you to remember that you have been loved. You may even"—and she smiled very gently, with a tender wry humor on her face—"marry some Mizzer girl because her body or her face or her manner reminds me to you."

"In a week—?" he gasped.

"Less than that."

"Who are you," he cried out, "that you, an underperson, should run real people and should manipulate their lives?"

"I didn't look for power, Casher. Power doesn't usually work if you look for it. I have eighty-nine thousand years to live, Casher, and as long as my master lives, I shall love him and take care of him. Isn't he handsome? Isn't he wise? Isn't he the most perfect master you ever saw?"

Casher thought of the old ruined-looking body with the plastic knobs set into it; he thought of the faded pajama bottoms; he said nothing.

"You don't have to agree," said T'ruth. "I know I have a special way of looking at him. But they took my turtle brain and raised the IQ to above normal human level. They took me when I was a happy little girl, enchanted by the voice and the glance and the touch of my master—they took me to where this real woman lay dying and they put me into a machine and they put her into one, too. When they were through, they picked me up. I had on a pink dress with pastel blue socks and pink shoes. They carried me out into the corridor, on a rug. They had finished with me. They knew that I wouldn't die. I was healthy. Can't you see it, Casher? I cried myself to sleep, nine hundred years ago."

Casher could not really answer. He nodded sympathetically.

"I was a girl, Casher. Maybe I was a turtle once, but I don't remember that, any more than you remember your mother's womb or your laboratory bottle. In that one hour I was never to be a girl again. I did not need to go to school. I had *her* education, and it was a good one. She spoke twenty or more languages. She was a psychologist and a hypnotist and a strategist. She was also the tyrannical mistress of this house. I cried because my childhood was finished, because I knew what I would have to do. I cried because I knew that I could do it. I *loved* my master so, but I was no longer to be

the pretty little servant who brought him his tablets or his
sweetmeats or his beer. Now I saw the truth—as she died I
had myself become Henriada. The planet was mine to care
for, to manage—to protect my master. If I come along and I
protect and help you, is that so much for a woman who will
just be growing up when your grandchildren will all be dead
of old age?"

"No, no," stammered Casher O'Neill. "But your own
life? A family, perhaps?"

Anger lashed across her pretty face. Her features were the
features of the delicious girl-child T'ruth, but her expression was that of the citizeness Agatha Madigan, perhaps, a
worldly woman reborn to the endless worldliness of her
own wisdom.

"Should I order a husband from the turtle bank, perhaps?
Should I hire out a piece of my master's estate, to be sold to
somebody because I'm an underperson, or perhaps put to
work somewhere in an industrial ship? I'm *me*. I may be an
animal, but I have more civilization in me than all the wind-
people on this planet. Poor things! What kind of people are
they, if they are only happy when they catch a big mutated
duck and tear it to pieces, eating it raw? I'm not going to
lose, Casher. I'm going to win. My master will live longer
than any person has ever lived before. He gave me that
mission when he was strong and wise and well in the prime
of his life. I'm going to do what I was made for, Casher, and
you're going to go back to Mizzer and make it free, whether
you like it or not!"

They both heard a happy scurrying on the staircase.

The small silver robot, little Harry Hadrian, burst upon
them; he carried a teaching helmet.

T'ruth said, "Resume your post. You are a good boy,
little Harry, and you can have time to sit in the garden later
on, when it is safe."

"Can I sit in a tree?" the little robot asked.

"Yes, if it is safe."

Little Harry Hadrian resumed his post by the gun cabinet. He kept the key in his hand. It was a very strange key, sharp at the end and as long as an awl. Casher supposed that it must be one of the straight magnetic keys, cued to its lock by a series of magnetized patterns.

"Sit on the floor for a minute," said T'ruth to Casher; "you're too tall for me." She slipped the helmet on his head, adjusted the levers on each side so that the helmet sat tight and true upon his skull.

With a touching gesture of intimacy, for which she gave him a sympathetic apologetic little smile, she moistened the two small electrodes with her own spit, touching her finger to her tongue and then to the electrode. These went to his temples.

She adjusted the verniered dials on the helmet itself, lifted the rear wire and applied it to her forehead.

Casher heard the click of a switch.

"That did it," he heard T'ruth's voice saying, very far away.

He was too busy looking into the gun cabinet. He knew them all and loved some of them. He knew the feel of their stocks on his shoulder, the glimpse of their barrels in front of his eyes, the dance of the target on their various sights, the welcome heavy weight of the gun on his supporting arm, the rewarding thrust of the stock against his shoulder when he fired. He knew all this, and did not know how he knew it.

"The Hechizera, Agatha herself, was a very accomplished sportswoman," murmured T'ruth to him. "I thought her knowledge would take a second printing when I passed it along to you. Let's take these."

She gestured to little Harry Hadrian, who unlocked the cabinet and took out two enormous guns, which looked like the long muskets mankind had had on earth even before the age of space began.

"If you're going to shoot children," said Casher with his

new-found expertness, "these won't do. They'll tear the bodies completely to pieces."

T'ruth reached into the little bag which hung from her belt. She took out three shotgun shells. "I have three more," she said. "Six children is all we need."

Casher looked at the slug projecting slightly from the shotgun casing. It did not look like any shell he had ever seen before. The workmanship was unbelievably fine and precise.

"What are they? I never saw these before."

"Proximity stunners," she said. "Shoot ten centimeters above the head of any living thing and the stunner knocks it out."

"You want the children alive?"

"Alive, of course. And unconscious. They are a part of your final test."

Two hours later, after an exciting hike to the edge of the weather controls, they had the six children stretched out on the floor of the great hall. Four were little boys, two girls; they were fine-boned, soft-haired people, very thin, but they did not look too far from earth-normal.

T'ruth called up a doctor-underman from among her servants. There must have been a crowd of fifty or sixty undermen and robots standing around. Far up the staircase, John Joy Tree stood hidden, half in shadow. Casher suspected that he was as inquisitive as the others but afraid of himself, Casher, "the man of blood."

T'ruth spoke quietly but firmly to the doctor. "Can you give them a strong euphoric before you waken them? We don't want to have to pluck them out of all the curtains in the house, if they go wild when they wake up."

"Nothing simpler," said the doctor-underman. He seemed to be of dog origin, but Casher could not tell.

He took a glass tube and touched it to the nape of each little neck. The necks were all streaked with dirt. These children had never been washed in their lives, except by the rain.

"Wake them," said T'ruth.

The doctor stepped back to a rolling table. It gleamed with equipment. He must have pre-set his devices, because all he did was to press a button and the children stirred into life.

The first reaction was wildness. They got ready to bolt. The biggest of the boys, who by earth-standards would have been about ten, got three steps before he stopped and began laughing.

T'ruth spoke the Old Common Tongue to them, very slowly and with long spaces between the words:

"Wind-children—do—you—know—where—you—are?"

The biggest girl twittered back to her so fast that Casher could not understand it.

T'ruth turned to Casher and said, "The girl said that she is in the Dead Place, where the air never moves and where the Old Dead Ones move around on their own business. She means us." To the wind-children she spoke again.

"What—would—you—like—most?"

The biggest girl went from child to child. They nodded agreement vigorously. They formed a circle and began a little chant. By the second repetition around, Casher could make it out.

> Shig—shag—shuggery,
> > shuck shuck shuck!
> What all of us need is
> > an all-around duck.
> Shig—shag—shuggery,
> > shuck shuck shuck!

At the fourth or fifth repetition they all stopped and looked at T'ruth, who was so plainly the mistress of the house. She in turn spoke to Casher O'Neill: "They think that they want a tribal feast of raw duck. What they are going to get is inoculations against the worst diseases of this planet, several duck meals, and their freedom again. But they need something else beyond all measure. *You know what that is, Casher, if you can only find it.*"

The whole crowd turned its eyes on Casher, the human eyes of the people and the underpeople, the milky lenses of the robots.

Casher stood aghast.

"Is this a test?" he asked, softly.

"You could call it that," said T'ruth, looking away from him.

Casher thought furiously and rapidly. It wouldn't do any good to make them into forgetties. The household had enough of them. T'ruth had announced a plan to let them loose again. Mister and owner Murray Madigan must have told her, sometime or other, to "do something" about the wind-people. She was trying to do it. The whole crowd watched him. What might T'ruth expect?

The answer came to him in a flash.

If she were asking *him,* it must be something to do with himself, something which he—uniquely among these people, underpeople and robots—had brought to the storm-sieged mansion of Beauregard.

Suddenly he saw it.

"Use me, my lady Ruth," said he, deliberately giving her the wrong title, "to print on them nothing from my intellectual knowledge, but everything from my emotional makeup. It wouldn't do them any good to know about Mizzer, where the Twelve Niles work their way down across the Intervening Sands. Not about Pontoppidan, the Gem Planet. Nor about Olympia, where the blind brokers promenade under numbered clouds. Knowing things would not help these children. But *wanting*—"

He was unique. He had wanted to return to Mizzer. He had wanted return beyond all dreams of blood and revenge.

He had wanted things fiercely, wildly, so that even if he could not get them, he zig-zagged the galaxy in search of them.

T'ruth was speaking to him again, urgently and softly, but not in so low a voice that the others in the room could not hear.

"And what, Casher O'Neill, should I give them from you?"

"My emotional structure. My determination. My desire. Nothing else. Give them that and throw them back into the winds. Perhaps if they want something fiercely enough, they will grow up to find out what it is."

There was a soft murmur of approval around the room.

T'ruth hesitated a moment and then nodded. "You answered, Casher. You answered quickly and perceptively. Bring seven helmets, Eunice. Stay here, doctor."

Eunice, the forgetty, left, taking two robots with her.

"A chair," said T'ruth to no one in particular. "For him."

A large powerful underman pushed his way through the crowd and dragged a chair to the end of the room.

T'ruth gestured that Casher should sit in it.

She stood in front of him. *Strange,* thought Casher, *that she should be a great lady and still a little girl.* How would he ever find a girl like her? He was not even afraid of the mystery of the Fish, or the image of the man on two pieces of wood. He no longer dreaded space-three, where so many travelers had gone in and so few had come out. He felt safe, comforted by her wisdom and authority. He felt that he would never see the likes of this again—a child running a planet and doing it well; a half-dead man surviving through the endless devotion of his maidservant; a fierce woman hypnotist living on with all the anxieties and angers of humanity gone, but with the skill and obstinacy of turtle genes to sustain her in her re-imprinted form.

"I can guess what you are thinking," said T'ruth, "but

we have already said the things that we had to say. I've peeped your mind a dozen times and I know that you want to go back to Mizzer so bad that space-three will spit you out right at the ruined fort where the big turn of the Seventh Nile begins. In my own way I love you, Casher, but I could not keep you here without turning you into a forgetty and making you a servant to my master. You know what always comes first with me, and always will."

"Madigan."

"Madigan," she answered, and with her voice the name itself was a prayer.

Eunice came back with the helmets.

"When we are through with these, Casher, I'll have them take you to the conditioning room. Good-bye, my might-have-been!"

In front of everyone, she kissed him full on the lips.

He sat in the chair, full of patience and contentment. Even as his vision blacked out, he could see the thin light sheath of a smock on the girlish figure, he could remember the tender laughter lurking in her smile.

In the last instant of his consciousness, he saw that another figure had joined the crowd—the tall old man with the worn bathrobe, the faded blue eyes, the thin yellow hair. Murray Madigan had risen from his private-life-in-death and had come to see the last of Casher O'Neill. He did not look weak, nor foolish. He looked like a great man, wise and strange in ways beyond Casher's understanding.

There was the touch of T'ruth's little hand on his arm and everything became a velvety cluttered dark quiet inside his own mind.

XIV

When he awoke, he lay naked and sunburned under the hot sky of Mizzer. Two soldiers with medical patches were rolling him on to a canvas litter.

"Mizzer!" he cried to himself. His throat was too dry to make a sound. "I'm home."

Suddenly the memories came to him and he scrabbled and snatched at them, seeing them dissolve within his mind before he could get paper to write them down.

Memory: there was the front hall, himself getting ready to sleep in the chair, with the old giant of Murray Madigan at the edge of the crowd and the tender light touch of T'ruth—his girl, his girl, now uncountable light-years away—putting her hand on his arm.

Memory: there was another room, with stained glass pictures and incense, and the weepworthy scenes of a great life shown in frescoes around the wall. There were the two pieces of wood and man in pain nailed to them. But Casher knew that scattered and coded through his mind, there was the ultimate and undefeatable wisdom of the sign of the Fish. He knew he could never fear fear again.

Memory: there was a gaming table in a bright room, with the wealth of a thousand worlds being raked toward him. He was a woman, strong, big-busted, bejewelled and proud. He was Agatha Madigan, winning at the games. (*That must have come,* he thought, *when they printed me with T'ruth.*) And in that mind of the Hechizera, which was now his own

129

mind, too, there was clear sure knowledge of how he could win men and women, officers and soldiers, even underpeople and robots, to his cause without a drop of blood or word of anger.

The man, lifting him on the litter, made red waves of heat and pain roll over him.

He heard one of them say, "Bad case of burn. Wonder how he lost his clothes."

The words were matter-of-fact; the comment was nothing special; but the cadence, that special cadence, was the true speech of Mizzer.

As they carried him away, he remembered the face of Rankin Meiklejohn, enormous eyes staring with inward despair over the brim of a big glass. That was the Administrator. On Henriada. That was the man who sent me past Ambiloxi to Beauregard at two seventy-five in the morning. The litter jolted a little.

He thought of the wet marshes of Henriada and knew that soon he would never remember them again. The worms of the tornadoes creeping up to the edge of the estate. The mad wise face of John Joy Tree.

Space three? Space three? Already, even now, he could not remember how they had put him into space three.

And space three itself—

All the nightmares which mankind has ever had pushed into Casher's mind. He twisted once in agony, just as the litter reached a medical military cart. He saw a girl's face— what *was* her name?—and then he slept.

XV

Fourteen Mizzer days later, the first test came.

A doctor colonel and an intelligence colonel, both in the workaday uniform of Colonel Wedder's Special Forces, stood by his bed.

"Your name is Casher O'Neill and we do not know how your body fell among the skirmishers," the doctor was saying, roughly and emphatically. Casher O'Neill turned his head on the pillow and looked at the man.

"Say something more!" he whispered to the doctor.

The doctor said, "You are a political intruder and we do not know how you got mixed up among our troops. We do not even know how you got back among the people of this planet. We found you on the Seventh Nile."

The intelligence colonel standing beside him, nodded agreement.

"Do you think the same thing, Colonel?" whispered Casher O'Neill to the intelligence colonel.

"I ask questions. I don't answer them," said the man gruffly.

Casher felt himself reaching for their minds with a kind of fingertip which he did not know he had. It was hard to put into ordinary words, but it felt as though someone had said to him, Casher: "That one is vulnerable at the left forefront area of his consciousness, but the other one is well armored and must be reached through the mid-brain." Casher was not afraid of revealing anything by his expression. He was too badly burned and in too much pain to show nuances of meaning on his face. (Somewhere he had heard of the wild story of the Hechizera of Gonfalon! Somewhere endless storms boiled across ruined marshes under a cloudy yellow sky! But where, when, what was that . . . ? He could not take time off for memory. He had to fight for his life.)

"Peace be with you," he whispered to both of them.

"Peace be with you," they responded in unison, with some surprise.

"Lean over me, please," said Casher, "so that I do not have to shout."

They stood stock straight.

Somewhere in the resources of his own memory and intelligence, Casher found the right note of pleading which could ride his voice like a carrier wave and make them do as he wished.

"This is Mizzer," he whispered.

"Of course this is Mizzer," snapped the intelligence colonel, "and you are Casher O'Neill. What are you doing here?"

"Lean over, gentlemen," he said softly, lowering his voice so that they could barely hear him.

This time, they did lean over.

His burned hands reached for their hands. The officers noticed it, but since he was sick and unarmed, they let him touch them.

Suddenly he felt their minds glowing in his as brightly as if he had swallowed their gleaming, thinking brains at a single gulp.

He spoke no longer.

He *thought* at them—torrential, irresistible thought.

I am not Casher O'Neill. You will find his body in a room, four doors down. I am the civilian Bindaoud.

The two colonels stared, breathing heavily.

Neither said a word.

Casher went on: "Our fingerprints and records have

gotten mixed. Give me the fingerprints and papers of the dead Casher O'Neill. Bury him then, quietly, but with honor. Once he loved your leader and there is no point in stirring up wild rumors about returns from out of space. I am Bindaoud. You will find my records in your front office. I am not a soldier. I am a civilian technician doing studies on the salt in blood chemistry under field conditions. You have heard me, gentlemen. You hear me now. You will hear me always. But you will not remember this, gentlemen, when you awaken. I am sick. You can give me water and a sedative."

They still stood, enraptured by the touch of his tight burned hands.

Casher O'Neill said, "Awaken."

Casher O'Neill let go their hands.

The medical colonel blinked and said amiably, "You'll be better, mister and doctor Bindaoud. I'll have the orderly bring you water and a sedative."

To the other officer he said, "I have an interesting corpse four doors down. I think you had better see it."

Casher O'Neill tried to think of the recent past, but the blue light of Mizzer was all around him, the sand-smell, the sound of horses galloping. For a moment, he thought of a big child's blue dress and he did not know why he almost wept.

Part Three

This is the story of the sand planet itself, Mizzer, which had lost all hope when the tyrant Wedder imposed the reign of terror and virtue. And its liberator, Casher O'Neill—of whom strange things were told, from the day of blood in which he fled from his native city of Kaheer, until he came back to end the shedding of blood for all the rest of his years.

Everywhere that Casher had gone, he had had only one thought in his mind—deliverance of his home country from the tyrants whom he himself had let slip into power when they had conspired against his uncle, the unspeakable Kuraf. He never forgot, whether waking or sleeping. He never forgot Kaheer itself along the First Nile, where the horses raced on the turf with the sand nearby. He never forgot the blue skies of his home and the great dunes of the desert between one Nile and the others. He remembered the freedom of a planet built and dedicated to freedom. He never forgot that the price of blood is blood, that the price of freedom is fighting, that the risk of fighting is death. But he was not a fool. He was willing if he had to, to risk his own death, but he wanted odds on the battle which would not merely snare him home, like a rabbit to be caught in a steel trap, by the police of the dictator Wedder.

And then, he met the solution of his crusade without knowing it at first. He had come to the end of all things, all problems, all worries. He had also come to the end of all ordinary hope. He met T'ruth. Now her subtle powers belonged to Casher O'Neill, to do with as he pleased.

It pleased him to return to Mizzer, to enter Kaheer itself, and to confront Wedder.

Why should he not come? It was his home and he thirsted for revenge. More than revenge he hungered for justice. He had lived many years for this hour and this hour came.

He entered the north gate of Kaheer.

I

Casher walked into Mizzer wearing the uniform of a medical technician in Wedder's own military service. He had assumed the appearance and the name of a dead man named Bindaoud. Casher walked with nothing more than his hands as weapons, and his hands swung freely at the end of his arms. Only the steadfastness of his feet, the resolute grace with which he took each step, betrayed his purpose. The crowds in the street saw him pass but they did not see him. They looked at a man and they did not realize that they saw their own history going step by step through their various streets. Casher O'Neill had entered the city of Kaheer; he knew that he was being followed. He could feel it.

He glanced around.

He had learned in his many years of fighting and struggle, on strange planets, countless rules of unremembered hazards. To be alert, he knew what this was. It was a suchesache. The suchesache at the moment had taken the shape of a small witless boy, some eight years old, who had two trails of stained mucus pouring down from his nostrils, who had forever-open lips ready to call with the harsh bark of idiocy, who had eyes that did not focus right. Casher O'Neill knew that this was a boy and not a boy. It was a hunting and searching device often employed by police lords when they presumed to make themselves into kings or tyrants, a device which flitted from shape to shape, from child to butterfly or bird, which moved with the suchesache and watched the victim; watching, saying nothing, following. He hated the suchesache and was tempted to throw all the powers of his strange mind at it so that the boy might die and the machine hidden within it might perish. But he knew that this would lead to a cascade of fire and splashing of blood. He had already seen blood in Kaheer long ago; he had no wish to see it in the city again.

Instead he stopped the pacing which had been following his cadenced walk through the street. He turned calmly and kindly and looked at the boy, and he said to the boy and to the hideous machine within the boy, "Come along with me; I'm going straightway to the palace and you would like to see that."

The machine, confronted, had no further choice.

The idiot boy put his hand in Casher's hand and somehow or other Casher O'Neill managed to resume the rolling deliberate march which had marked so many of his years, while keeping a grip on the hand of the demented child who skipped beside him. Casher would still feel the machine watching him from within the eyes of the boy. He did not care; he was not afraid of guns, he could stop them. He was not afraid of poison; he could resist it. He was not afraid of hypnotism; he could take it in and spit it back. He was not afraid of fear; he had been on Henriada. He had come home through space-three. There was nothing left to fear.

Straightway went he to the palace. The midday gleamed in the bright yellow sun which rode the skies of Kaheer. The whitewashed walls in the arabesque design stayed as they had been for thousands of years. Only at the door was he challenged, but the sentry hesitated as Casher spoke:

"I am Bindaoud, loyal servant to Colonel Wedder, and this is a child of the streets whom I propose to heal in order to show our good Colonel Wedder a fair demonstration of my powers."

The sentry said something into a little box which sat in the wall.

Casher passed freely. The suchesache trotted beside him. As he went through the corridors, laid with rich rugs, military and civilians moving back and forth, he felt happy. This was not the palace of Wedder, though Wedder lived in it. It was his own palace. He, Casher, had been born in it. He knew it. He knew every corridor.

The changes of the years were very few. Casher turned left into an open courtyard. He smelled the smell of salt water and the sand and the horses nearby. He sighed a little at the familiarity of it, the good and kind welcome. He turned right again and ascended long, long stairs. Each step was carpeted in a different design.

His uncle Kuraf had stood at the head of these very stairs while men and women, boys and girls were brought to him to become toys of his evil pleasures. Kuraf had been too fat to walk down these stairs to greet them. He always let the captives come up to himself and to his den of pleasures. Casher reached the top of the stairs and turned left.

This was no den of pleasures now.

It was the office of Colonel Wedder. He, Casher, had reached it.

How strange it was to reach this office, this target of all his hopes, this one fevered pinpoint in all the universe for which his revenge had thirsted until he thought himself mad. He had thought of bombing this office from outer space, or of cutting it with the thin arc of a laser beam, or of poisoning it with chemicals, of assaulting it with troops. He had thought of pouring fire on this building, or water. He had dreamed of making Mizzer free—even at the price of the lovely city of Kaheer itself—by finding a small asteroid somewhere and crashing it, in an interplanetary tragedy, directly into the city itself. And the city, under the roar of that impact, would have blazed into thermonuclear incandescence and would have become a poison lake at the end of the Twelve Niles. He had thought of a thousand ways of entering the city and of destroying the city, merely in order to destroy Wedder. Now he was here. So too was Wedder.

Wedder did not know that he, Casher O'Neill, had come back.

Even less did Wedder know who Casher O'Neill had become, the master of space, the traveler who traveled without ships, the vehicle for devices stranger than any mind on Mizzer had ever conceived.

Very calm, very relaxed, very quiet, very assured, the doom which was Casher O'Neill walked into the antechamber of Wedder. Very modestly, he asked for Wedder.

The dictator happened to be free.

He had changed little since Casher last saw him, a little older, a little fatter, a little wiser—all these perhaps. Casher was not sure. Every cell and filament in his living body had risen to the alert. He was ready to do the work for which the light-years had ached, for which the worlds had turned, and he knew that within an instant it would be done. He confronted Wedder, gave Wedder a modest assured smile.

"Your servant, the technician Bindaoud, sir and colonel," said Casher O'Neill. Wedder looked at him strangely. He reached out his hand, and, even as their hands touched, Wedder said the last words he would ever say on his own. Within that handclasp, Wedder spoke again and his voice was strange:

"Who are you?"

Casher had dreamed that he would say, "I am Casher O'Neill come back from unimaginable distances to punish you," or that he would say, "I am Casher O'Neill and I have ridden star-lanes for years upon years to find your destruction." Or he had even thought that he might say, "Surrender or die, Wedder, your time has come." Sometimes he had dreamed he would say, "Here, Wedder," and then show him the knife with which to take his blood.

Yet this was the climax and none of these things occurred.

The idiot boy with the machine within it stood at ease.

Casher O'Neill merely held Wedder's hand and said quite simply, "Your friend."

As he said that, he searched back and forth. He could feel inner eyes within his own head, eyes which did not move within the sockets of his face, eyes which he did not have and with which he could nevertheless see. These were the eyes of his perception. Quickly, he adjusted the anatomy of Wedder, working kinesthetically, squeezing an artery there, pinching off a gland here. Here, harden the tissue, through which the secretions of a given endocrine material had to come. In less time than it would take an ordinary doctor to describe the process, he had changed Wedder. Wedder had been tuned down like a radio with dials realigned, like a spaceship with its locksheets reset.

The work which Casher had done was less than any pilot does in the course of an ordinary landing; but the piloting he had done was within the biochemical system of Wedder himself. And the changes which he had effected were irreversible.

The new Wedder was the old Wedder. The same mind. The same will, the same personality. Yet its permutations were different. And its method of expression already slightly different. More benign. More tolerant. More calm, more human. Even a little corrupt, as he smiled and said, "I remember you, now, Bindaoud. Can you help that boy?"

The supposed Bindaoud ran his hands over the boy. The boy wept with pain and shock for a moment. He wiped his dirty nose and upper lip on his sleeves. His eyes came into focus. His lips compressed. His mind burned brightly as its old worn channels became human instead of idiot. The suchesache machine knew it was out of place and fled for another refuge. The boy, given his brains, but no words, no education yet, stood there and hiccuped with joy. Wedder said very pleasantly, "That is remarkable. Is it all that you have to show me?"

"All," said Casher O'Neill, "you were not he."

He turned his back on Wedder and did so in perfect safety.

He knew Wedder would never kill another man.

Casher stopped at the door and looked back. He could tell from the posture of Wedder that that which had to be done, had been done: the changes within the man were larger than the man himself. The planet was free and Casher's own work was indeed done. The suddenly frightened child, which had lost the suchesache, followed him out of blind instinct.

The colonels and the staff officers did not know whether to salute or nod when they saw their chief stand at the doorway, and waved with unexpected friendliness at Casher O'Neill as Casher descended the broad carpeted steps, the child stumbling after him. At the furthest steps, Casher looked one last time at the enemy who had become almost a part of himself. There stood Wedder, the man of blood. And now, he himself, Casher O'Neill, had expunged the blood, had redone the past, and reshaped the future. All Mizzer was heading back to the openness and freedom which it had enjoyed in the time of the old Republic of the Twelve Niles. He walked on, shifting from one corridor to the other and using short-cuts to the courtyards, until he came to the doorway of the palace. The sentry presented arms.

"At ease," said Casher. The man put down his gun. Casher stood outside the palace, that palace which had been his uncle's, which had been his own, which had really been himself. He felt the clear air of Mizzer. He looked at the clear blue skies which he had always loved. He looked at the world to which he had promised he would return, with justice, with vengeance, with thunder, with power. Thanks to the strange and subtle capacities which he had learned from the turtle-girl, T'ruth, hidden in her own world amid the storm-churned atmosphere of Henriada, he had not needed to fight.

Casher turned to the boy and said, "I am a sword which has been put in its scabbard. I am a pistol with the cartridges dropped out. I am a wirepoint with no battery behind it. I am a man, but I am very empty."

The boy made strangled, confused sounds as though he were trying to think, to become himself, to make up for all the lost time he had spent in idiocy.

Casher acted on impulse. Curiously, he gave to the boy his own native speech of Kaheer. He felt his muscles go tight, shoulder, neck, fingertips, as he concentrated with the arts he had learned in the palace of Beauregard where the girl T'ruth governed almost-forever in the name of Mister and Owner Murray Madigan. He took the arts and memories he sought. He seized the boy roughly but tightly by the shoulders. He peered into frightened crying eyes and then, in a single blast of thought, he gave the boy speech, memory, ambition, skills. The boy stood there dazed.

At last the boy spoke and he asked, "Who am I?"

Casher could not answer that one. He patted the child on the shoulder. He said, "Go back to the city and find out. I have other needs. I have to find out who I myself may be. Good-bye and peace be with you."

II

Casher remembered that his mother still lived here. He had often forgotten her. It would have been easier to forget her. Her name was Trihaep, and she had been sister to Kuraf. Where Kuraf had been vicious, she had been virtuous. Where Kuraf had sometimes been grateful, she had been thrifty and shifty. Where Kuraf, with all his evils, had acquired a toleration for men and things and ideas, she remained set on the pattern of thought which her parents had long ago taught her.

Casher O'Neill did something he thought he would never do. He had never really even thought about doing it. It was too simple. He went home.

At the gate of the house, his mother's old servant knew him, despite the change in his face and she said, with a terrible awe in her voice, "It seems to me that I am looking at Casher O'Neill."

"I use the name, Bindaoud," said Casher, "but I am Casher O'Neill. Let me in and tell my mother that I am here."

He went into the private apartment of his mother. The old furniture was still there. The polished bricabrac of a hundred ages, the old paintings and the old mirrors, and the dead people whom he had never known, represented by their pictures and their mementoes. He felt just as ill at ease as he felt when he was a small boy, when he had visited the same room, before his uncle came to take him to the palace.

His mother came in. She had not changed.

He half-thought that she would reach out her arms to him, and cry in a deliberately modern passion, "My baby! My precious! Come back to me!"

She did no such thing.

She looked at him coldly as though he were a complete stranger.

She said to him, "You don't look like my son, but I suppose that you are. You have made trouble enough in your time. Are you making trouble now?"

"I make no malicious trouble, Mother, and I never have," said Casher, "no matter what you may think of me. I did what I had to do. I did what was right."

"Betraying your uncle was right? Letting down our family was right? Disgracing us all was right? You must be a fool to talk like this. I heard that you were a wanderer, that you had great adventures, and had seen many worlds. You don't sound any different to me. You're an old man. You almost seem as old as I do. I had a baby once, but how could that be you? You are an enemy of the house of Kuraf O'Neill. You're one of the people who brought it down in blood. But they came from outside with their principles and their thoughts and their dreams of power. And you stole from inside like a cur. You opened the door and you let in ruin. Who are you that I should forgive you?"

"I do not ask your forgiveness, Mother," said Casher. "I do not even ask your understanding. I have other places to go and other things yet to do. May peace be upon you."

She stared at him, said nothing.

He went on, "You will find Mizzer a more pleasant place to live in, since I talked to Wedder this morning."

"You talked to Wedder?" cried she. "And he did not kill you?"

"He did not know me."

"Wedder did not know you?"

"I assure you, Mother, he did not know me."

"You must be a very powerful man, my son. Perhaps you can repair the fortune of the house of Kuraf O'Neill after all the harm you have done, and all the heartbreak you brought to my brother. I suppose you know your wife's dead?"

"I had heard that," said Casher. "I hope she died instantly in an accident and without pain."

"Of course it was an accident. How else do people die these days? She and her husband tried out one of those new boats and it overturned."

"I'm sorry, I wasn't there."

"I know that. I know that perfectly well, my son. You were outside there, so that I had to look up at the stars with fear. I could look up in the sky and stare for the man who was my son lurking up there with blood and ruin. With vengeance upon vengeance heaped upon all of us, just because he thought he knew what was right. I've been afraid of you for a long long time, and I thought if I ever met you again I would fear you with my whole heart. You don't quite seem to be what I expected, Casher. Perhaps I can like you. Perhaps I can even love you as a mother should. Not that it matters. You and I are too old now."

"I'm not working on that kind of mission any longer, Mother. I have been in this old room long enough and I wish you well. But I wish many other people well, too. I have done what I had to do. Perhaps I had better say good-bye, and much later perhaps, I will come back and see you again. When both of us know more about what we have to do."

"Don't you even want to see your daughter?"

"Daughter?" said Casher O'Neill. "Do I have a daughter?"

"Oh, poor fool, you. Didn't you even find that out after you left? She bore your child, all right. She even went through the old-fashioned business of a natural birth. The child even looks something like the way you used to look. Matter of fact, she's rather arrogant, like you. You can call on her if you want to. She lives in the house which is just outside the square in Golden Laut in the leather workers' area. Her husband's name is Ali Ali. Look her up if you want to."

She extended a hand. Casher took the hand as though she had been a queen. And he kissed the cool fingers. As he looked her in the face, here, too, he brought his skills from Henriada in place. He surveyed and felt her personality as though he were a surgeon of the soul, but in this case there was nothing for him to do. This was not a dynamic personality struggling and fighting and moving against the forces of life and hope and disappointment. This was something else, a person set in life, immobile, determined, rigid even for a man with healing arts who could destroy a fleet with his thoughts or who could bring an idiot to normality by mere command. He could see that this was a case beyond his powers.

He patted the old hand affectionately and she smiled warmly at him, not knowing what it meant. "If anyone asks," said Casher, "the name I have been using is that of the Doctor Bindaoud. Bindaoud the technician. Can you remember that, Mother?"

"Bindaoud the technician," she echoed, as she led him out the door to walk in the street.

Within twenty minutes he was knocking at his daughter's door.

III

The daughter herself answered the door. She flung it open. She looked at the strange man, surveyed him from head to heels. She noted the medical insignia on his uniform. She noted his mark of rank. She appraised him shrewdly, quickly, and she knew he had no business there in the quarters of the leather workers.

"Who are you?" she sang out, quickly and clearly.

"In these hours and at this time, I pass under the name of the expert Bindaoud, a technician and medical man back from the special forces of Colonel Wedder. I'm just on leave, you see, but sometime later, madam, you might find out who I really am and I thought you better hear it from my lips. I'm your father."

She did not move. The significant thing is that she did not move at all. Casher studied her and could see the cast of his own bones in the shape of her face, could see the length of his own fingers repeated in her hands. He had sensed that the storms of duty which had blown him from sorrow to sorrow, the wind of consciousness which had kept alive his dreams of vengeance, had turned into something very different in her. It, too, was a force, but not the kind of force he understood.

"I have children now and I would just as soon you not meet them. As a matter of fact, you have never done me a good deed except to beget me. You have never done me an ill deed except to threaten my life from beyond the stars. I am tired of you and I am tired of everything you were or might have been. Let's forget it. Can't you go your way and let me be? I may be your daughter, but I can't help that."

"As you wish, madam. I have had many adventures and I do not propose to tell them to you. I can see quickly enough that you have what is seemingly a good life, and I hope that my deeds this morning in the palace will have made it better. You'll find out soon enough. Good-bye."

The door closed upon him and he walked back through the sun-drenched market of the leather workers. There were golden hides there. Hides of animals which had then been artfully engraved with very fine strips of beaten gold so that they gleamed in the sunlight. Casher looked upward and around.

Where do I go now? thought he. *Where do I go when I've done everything I had to do? When I've loved everyone I have wanted to love, when I have been everything I have had to be? What does a man with a mission do when the mission is fulfilled? Who can be more hollow than a victor? If I had lost, I could still want revenge. But I haven't. I've won. And I've won nothing. I've wanted nothing for myself from this dear city. I want nothing from this dear world. It's not in my power to give it or to take it. Where do I go when I have nowhere to go? What do I become when I am not ready for death and I have no reason whatsoever for life?*

There sprang into his mind the memory of the world of Henriada with the twisting snakes of the little tornadoes. He could see the slender, pale, hushed face of the girl T'ruth and he remembered at last that which it was which she had held in her hand. It was the magic. It was the secret sign of the old, strong religion. There was the man forever dying nailed to two pieces of wood. It was the mystery behind the civilization of all these stars. It was the thrill of the First Forbidden One, the Second Forbidden One, the Third Forbidden One. It was the mystery on which the robot, rat, and Copt agreed when they came back from space-three. He knew what he had to do.

He could not find himself because there was no himself to be found. He was a used tool. A discarded vessel. He was a shard tossed on the ruins of time, and yet he was a man with eyes and brains to think and with many unaccustomed powers.

He reached into the sky with his mind, calling for a public flying machine. "Come and get me," he said, and the great winged birdlike machine came soaring over the rooftops and dropped gently into the square.

"I thought I heard you call, sir."

Casher reached into his pocket and took out his imaginary pass signed by Wedder, authorizing him to use all the vehicles of the republic in the secret service of the regime of Colonel Wedder. The sergeant recognized the pass and almost popped out his eyes in respect.

"The Ninth Nile, can you reach it with this machine?"

"Easily," said the sergeant. "But you better get some shoes first. Iron shoes because the ground there is mostly volcanic glass."

"Wait here for me," said Casher. "Where can I get the shoes?"

"Two streets over and better get two water bottles, too."

IV

Within a matter of minutes he was back. The sergeant watched him fill the bottles in the fountain. He looked at his medical insignia without doubt and showed him how to sit on the cramped emergency seat inside the great machine bird. They snapped their seat belts and the sergeant said, "Ready?" and the ornithopter spread out its wings, and flew into the air.

The huge wings were like oars digging into a big sea. They rose rapidly and soon Kaheer was below them, the fragile minarets and the white sand with the racing turf along the river, and the green fields, and even the pyramids copied from something on Ancient Earth.

The operator did something and the machine flew harder. The wings, although far slower than any jet aircraft, were steady, and they moved with respectable speed across the broad dry desert. Casher still wore his decimal watch from Henriada and it was two whole decimal hours before the sergeant turned around, pinched him gently awake from the drowse into which he had fallen, shouted something and pointed down. A strip of silver matched by two strips of green wandering through a wilderness of black, gleaming glittering black, with the beige sands of the everlasting desert stretching everywhere in the distance.

"The Ninth Nile?" shouted Casher. The sergeant smiled the smile of a man who had heard nothing but wanted to be agreeable, and the ornithopter dived with a lurching suddenness toward the twist in the river. A few buildings became visible. They were modest and small. Verandas, perhaps, for the use of a visitor. Nothing more.

It was not the sergeant's business to query anyone on secret orders from Colonel Wedder. He showed the cramped Casher O'Neill how to get out of the ornithopter, and then, standing in his seat, saluted, and said, "Anything else, sir?"

Casher said, "No. I'll make my own way. If they ask you who I was, I am the Doctor Bindaoud and you have left me here under orders."

"Right, sir," said the sergeant, and the great machine reached out its gleaming wings, flapped, spiraled, climbed, became a dot and vanished.

Casher stood there alone. Utterly alone. For many years he had been supported by a sense of purpose, by a drive to do something, and now the drives and the purpose were gone, and his life was gone, and the use of his future was gone, and he had nothing. All he had was the ultimate imagination, health, and great skills. These were not what he wanted. He wanted the liberation of all Mizzer. But he had gotten that, so what was it? He almost stumbled towards one of the nearby buildings.

A voice spoke up. A woman's voice. The friendly voice of an old woman.

Very unexpectedly, she said, "I've been waiting for you, Casher; come on in."

V

He stared at her. "I've seen you," he said. "I've seen you somewhere. I know you well. You've affected my fate. You did something to me and yet I don't know who you are. How could you be here to meet me when I didn't know I was coming?"

"Everything in its time," said the woman. "With a time for everything and what you need now is rest. I'm D'alma, the dog-woman from Pontoppidan. The one who washed the dishes."

"Her," cried he.

"Me," she said.

"But you—but you—how did you get here?"

"I got here," she said. "Isn't that obvious?"

"Who sent you?"

"You're part of the way to the truth," she said. "You might as well hear a little more of it. I was sent here by a lord whose name I will never mention. A lord of the underpeople. Acting from earth. He sent out another dog-woman to take my place. And he had me shipped here as simple baggage. I worked in the hospital where you recovered and I read your mind as you got well. I knew what you would do to Wedder and I was pretty sure that you would come up here to the Ninth Nile, because that is the road that all searchers must take."

"Do you mean," he said, "that you know the road to—"

He hesitated and then plunged into his question, "the Holy of Unholies, the Thirteenth Nile?"

"I don't see that it means anything, Casher. Except that you'd better take off those iron shoes; you don't need them yet. You'd better come in here. Come on in."

He pushed the beaded curtains aside and entered the bungalow. It was a simple frontier official dwelling. There were cots hither and yon, a room to the rear which seemed to be hers; a dining room to the right and there were papers, a viewing machine, cards and games on the table. The room itself was astonishingly cool.

She said, "Casher, you've got to relax. And that is the hardest of all things to do. To relax, when you had a mission for many many years."

"I know it," said he. "I know it. But knowing it and doing it aren't the same things."

"Now you can do it," said D'alma.

"Do what?" he snapped.

"Relax, as we were talking about. All you have to do here is to have some good meals. Just sleep a few times, swim in the river if you want to. I have sent everyone away except myself, and you and I shall have this house. And I am an old woman, not even a human being. You're a man, a true man, who's conquered a thousand worlds. And who has finally triumphed over Wedder. I think we'll get along. And when you're ready for the trip, I'll take you."

The days did pass as she said they would. With insistent but firm kindness, she made him play games with her: simple, childish games with dice and cards. Once or twice he tried to hypnotize her. To throw the dice his own way. He changed the cards in her hand. He found that she had very little telepathic offensive power, but that her defenses were superb. She smiled at him whenever she caught him playing tricks. And his tricks failed.

With this kind of atmosphere he really began to relax.

She was the woman who had spelled happiness for him on Pontoppidan when he didn't know what happiness was. When he had abandoned the lovely Genevieve to go on with his quest for vengeance.

Once he said to her, "Is that old horse still alive?"

"Of course he is," she said. "That horse will probably outlive you and me. He thinks he's on Mizzer by galloping around a patrol capsule. Come on back; it's your turn to play."

He put down the cards, and slowly the peace, the simplicity, the reassuring, calm sweetness of it all stole over him and he began to perceive the nature of her therapy. It was to do nothing but slow him down. He was to meet himself again.

It may have been the tenth day, perhaps it was the fourteenth, that he said to her, "When do we go?"

She said, "I've been waiting for that question and we're ready now. We go."

"When?"

"Right now. Put on your shoes. You won't need them very much," she said, "but you might need them where we land. I am taking you part way there."

Within a few minutes, they went out into the yard. The river in which he had swum lay below. A shed, which he did not remember having noticed before, lay at the far end of the yard. She did something to the door, removing a lock, and the door flung open. And she pulled out a skeletonized ornithopter motor, wings, tails. The body was just a bracket of metal. The source of power was as usual an ultra-miniaturized, nuclear-powered battery. Instead of seats, there were two tiny saddles, like the saddle used in the bicycles of old, old Earth which he had seen in museums.

"You can fly that?" he asked.

"Of course I can fly it. It's better than going 200 miles over broken glass. We are leaving civilization now. We are leaving everything that was on any map. We are flying directly to the Thirteenth Nile, as you well knew it should be that."

"I knew that," he said. "I never expected to reach it so soon. Does this have anything to do with that Sign of the Fish you were talking about?"

"Everything, Casher. Everything. But everything in its place. Climb in behind me." He sat on top of the ornithopter and this one ran down the yard on its tall, graceful mechanical legs before the flaps of its wings put it in the air. She was a better pilot than the sergeant had been; she soared more and beat the wings less. She flew over country that he, a native of Mizzer, had never dreamed about.

They came to a city gaudy in color. He could see large fires burning alongside the river, and brightly painted people with their hands lifted in prayer. He saw temples and strange gods in them. He saw markets with goods, which he never though to see marketed.

"Where are we?" he asked.

D'alma said, "This is the City of Hopeless Hope." She put the ornithopter down and, as they climbed out of the saddles, it lifted itself into the air and flew back, in the direction from whence they had come. "You are staying with me?" asked Casher.

"Of course I am. I was sent to be with you."

"What for?"

"You are important to all the worlds, Casher, not just Mizzer. By the authority of the friends I have, they have sent me here to help you."

"But what do you get out of it?"

"I get nothing, Casher. I find my own destruction, perhaps, but I will accept that. Even the loss of my own hope if it only moves you further on in your voyage. Come, let us enter the city of Hopeless Hope."

VI

They walked through the strange streets. Almost everyone in the streets seemed to be engaged in the practice of religion. The stench of the burning dead was all round them. Talismans, luck charms, and funeral supplies were in universal abundance.

Casher said, speaking rather quietly to D'alma, "I never knew there was anything like this on any civilized planet."

"Obviously," she replied, "there must be many people who believe in worry about death; there are many who do know about this place. Otherwise there would not be the throngs here. These are the people who have the wrong hope and who go to no place at all, who find under this earth and under the stars their final fulfillment. These are the ones who are so sure that they are right that they never will be right. We must pass through them quickly, Casher, lest we, too, start believing."

No one impeded their passage in the streets, although many people paused to see that a soldier, even a medical soldier, in uniform, had the audacity to come there.

They were even more surprised that an old hospital attendant who seemed to be an off-world dog walked along beside him.

"We cross the bridge now, Casher, and this bridge is the most terrible thing I've ever seen, whereas now we are going to come to Jwindz and the Jwindz oppose you and me and everything you stand for."

"Who are the Jwindz?" asked Casher.

"The Jwindz are the perfect ones. They are perfect in this earth. You will see soon enough."

VII

As they crossed the bridge, a tall, blithe police official, clad in a neat black uniform, stepped up to them and said, "Go back. People from your city are not welcome here."

"We are not from that city," said D'alma. "We are travelers."

"Where are you bound?" asked the police official.

"We are bound for the source of the Thirteenth Nile."

"Nobody goes there," said the guard.

"*We* are going there," said D'alma.

"By what authority?"

Casher reached into his pocket and took out a genuine card. He had remade one, from the memories he had retained in his mind. It was an all-world pass, authorized by the Instrumentality.

The police official looked at it and his eyes widened.

"Sir and master, I thought you were merely one of Wedder's men. You must be someone of great importance. I will notify the scholars in the Hall of Learning at the middle of the city. They will want to see you. Wait here. A vehicle will come."

D'alma and Casher O'Neill did not have long to wait.

She said nothing at all in this time. Her air of good humor and competence ebbed perceptibly. She was distressed by the cleanliness and perfection around her, by the silence, by the dignity of the people.

When the vehicle came, it had a driver, as correct, as smooth, and as courteous as the guard at the bridge. He opened the door and waved them in. They climbed in and they sped noiselessly through the well-groomed streets: houses, each one in immaculate taste; trees, planted the way in which trees should be planted.

In the center square of the city, they stopped. The driver got out, walked around the vehicle, opened their door.

He pointed at the archway of the large building and he said, "They are expecting you."

Casher and D'alma walked up the steps reluctantly. She was reluctant because she had some sense of what this place was, a special dwelling for quiet doom and arrogant finality. He was reluctant because he could feel that in every bone of her body she resented this place. And he resented it, too.

They were led through the archway and across a patio to a large, elegant conference room.

Within the room a circular table had already been set in preparation of a meal.

Ten handsome men rose to greet them.

The first one said, "You are Casher O'Neill. You are the wanderer. You are the man dedicated to this planet and we appreciate what you have done for us, even though the power of Colonel Wedder never reached here."

"Thank you," said Casher. "I am surprised to hear that you know of me."

"That's nothing," said the man. "We know of everyone. And you, woman," said the same man to D'alma, "you know full well that we never entertain women here. And you are the only underperson in this city. A dog at that. But in honor of our guest we shall let you pass. Sit down if you wish. We want to talk to you."

A meal was served. Little squares of sweet unknown meat, fresh fruits, bits of melon, chased with harmonious drinks which cleared the mind and stimulated it, without intoxicating or drugging.

The language of their conversations was clear and elevated. All questions were answered swiftly, smoothly, and with positive clarity.

Finally, Casher was moved to ask, "I do not seem to have heard of you, Jwindz; who are you?"

"We are the perfect ones," said the oldest Jwindz. "We have all the answers; there is nothing else left to find."

"How do you get here?" said Casher.

"We are selected from many worlds."

"Where are your families?"

"We don't bring them with us."

"How do you keep out intruders?"

"If they are good, they wish to stay. If they are not good, we destroy them."

Casher—still shocked by his experience of fulfilling all his life's work in the confrontation with Wedder—though his life might be at stake, asked casually, "Have you decided yet whether I am perfect enough to join you? Or am I not perfect and to be destroyed?"

The heaviest of all the Jwindz, a tall, portly man, with a great bushy shock of black hair replied ponderously.

"Sir, you are forcing our decision, but I think that you may be something exceptional. We cannot accept you. There is too much force in you. You may be perfect, but you are more than perfect. We are men, sir, and I do not think that you are any longer a mere man. You are almost a machine. You are yourself dead people. You are the magic of ancient battles coming to strike among us. We are all of us a little afraid of you, and yet we do not know what to do with you. If you were to stay here a while, if you calmed down, we might give you hope. We know perfectly well what that dog-woman of yours calls our city. She calls it the city of Hopeless Hope. We just call it Jwindz Jo, in memory of the ancient Rule of the Jwindz, which somewhere once was obtained upon old Earth. And therefore, we think that we will neither kill you nor accept you. We think—do we not, gentlemen?—that we will speed you on your way, as we have sped no other traveler. And that we will send you, then, to a place which few people pass. But you have the strength and if you are going to the source of the Thirteenth Nile, you will need it."

"I will need strength?" Casher asked.

The first Jwindz who had met them at the door said, "Indeed you will need strength, if you go to Mortoval. We may be dangerous to the uninitiated. Mortoval is worse than dangerous. It is a trap many times worse than death. But go there if you must."

VIII

Casher O'Neill and D'alma reached Mortoval on a one-wheeled cart, which ran on a high wire past picturesque mountain gorges, soaring over two serrated series of peaks and finally dropping down to another bend in the same river, the illegal and forgotten Thirteenth Nile.

When the vehicle stopped, they got out. No one had accompanied them. The vehicle, held in place by gyroscopes and compasses, felt itself relieved of their weight and hurried home.

This time there was no city: just one great arch. D'alma clung close to him. She even took his arm and pulled it over her shoulder as though she needed protection. She whined a little as they walked up a low hill and finally reached the arch. They walked into the arch and a voice not made of sound cried out to them.

"I am youth and am everything that you have been or ever will be. Know this now before I show you more."

Casher was brave, and this time he was cheerfully hopeless, so he said, "I know who I am. Who are you?"

"I am the force of the Gunung Banga. I am the power of this planet which keeps everyone in this planet and which assures the order which persists among the stars, and promises that the dead shall not walk among the men. And I serve of the fate and the hope of the future. Pass if you think you can."

Casher searched with his own mind and he found what he wanted. He found the memory of a young child, T'ruth, who had been almost a thousand years on the planet of Henriada. A child, soft and gentle on the outside, but wise and formidable and terrible beyond belief, in the powers which she had carried, which had been imprinted upon her.

As he walked through the arch he cast the images of truth here and there. Therefore he was not one person but a multitude. And the machine and the living being, which hid behind the machine, the Gunung Banga, obviously could see him and could see D'alma walking through, but the machine was not prepared to recognize whole multitudes of crying throngs.

"Who are you thousands that you should come here now? Who are you multitudes that you should be two people? I sense all of you. The fighters and the ships and the men of blood, the searchers and the forgetters, there's even an Old North Australian renunciant here. And the great go-captain Tree, and there are even a couple of men of old Earth. You are all walking through me. How can I cope with you?"

"Make us, us," said Casher firmly.

"Make you, you," replied the machine. "Make you,

you. How can I make you, you, when I do not know who
you are, when you flit like ghosts and you confuse my
computers? There are too many, I say. There are too many
of you. It is ordained that you should pass."

"If it is so ordained, then let us pass." D'alma suddenly
stood proud and erect.

They walked on through.

She said, "You got us through." They had indeed passed
beyond the arch, and there, beyond the arch, lay a gentle
riverside with skiffs pulled up along the beach.

"This seems to be next," said Casher O'Neill.

D'alma nodded. "I'm your dog, master. We go where
you think."

They climbed into a skiff. Echoes of tumult followed
from the arch.

"Good-bye to troubles," the echoes said. "Had they
been people they would have been stopped. But she was a
dog and a servant, who had lived many years in the
happiness of the Sign of the Fish. And he was a combat-
ready man who had incorporated within himself the memories of adversaries and friends, too tumultuous for any
scanner to measure, too complex for any computer to
assess." The echoes resounded across the river.

There was even a dock on the other side. Casher tied the
skiff to the dock and he helped the dog-woman go toward
the buildings that they saw beyond some trees.

IX

D'alma said, "I have seen pictures of this place; this is the Kermesse Dorgüeil and here we may lose our way, because this is the place where all the happy things of this world come together, but where the man and the two pieces of wood never filter through. We shall see no one unhappy, no one sick, no one unbalanced; everyone will be enjoying the good things of life; perhaps I will enjoy it, too. May the Sign of the Fish help me that I not become perfect too soon."

"You won't be," Casher promised.

At the gate of this city, there was no guard at all. They walked on past a few people who seemed to be promenading outside the town. Within the city they approached what seemed to be a hotel and an inn or a hospital. At any rate it was a place where many people were fed.

A man came out and said, "Well, this is a strange sight; I never knew that the Colonel Wedder let his officers get this far from home, and as for you, Woman, you're not even a human being. You're an odd couple and you're not in love with each other. Can we do anything for you?"

Casher reached into his pocket and tossed several credit pieces of five denominations in front of the man.

"Don't these mean anything?" asked Casher.

Catching them in his fingers, the man said, "Oh, we can use money! We use it occasionally for important things; we don't need yours. We live well here, and we have a nice life, not like those two places across the river, which stay away from life. All men who are perfect are nothing but talk—Jwindz they call themselves, the perfect ones—well, we're not that perfect. We've got families and good friends and good clothes, and we get the latest news from all the worlds."

"News," said Casher, "I thought that was illegal."

"We get anything. You would be surprised at what we have here. It's a very civilized place. Come on in; this is the hotel of the Singing Swans and you can live here as long as you wish. When I say that, I mean it. Our treasure has unusual resources, and I can see that you are unusual people. You are not a medical technician, despite that uniform, and your follower is not a mere dog-underperson or you wouldn't have gotten this far."

They entered a promenade two stories high; little shops lined each side of the corridor with the treasures of the world on exhibit. The prices were marked explaining them, but there was no one in the stalls.

The smell of good food came from a cool dining room in the inn.

"Come into my office and have a drink. My name is Howard."

"That's an old Earth name," said Casher.

"Why shouldn't it be?" asked Howard. "I came here from old Earth. I looked for the best of all places, and it took me a long time to find it. This is it—the Kermesse Dorgüeil. We have nothing here but simple and clean pleasures; we have only those vices which help and support. We accomplish the possible; we reject the impossible. We live life, not death. Our talk is about things and not about ideas. We have nothing but scorn for that city behind you, the City of the Perfect Ones. And we have nothing but pity for the holier than holies far back where they claim to have Hopeless Hope, and practice nothing but evil religion. I passed through those places too, although I had to go around the city of the Perfect Ones. I know what they are and I've come all the way from Earth, and if I have come all the way from old old Earth I should know what this is. You should take my word for it."

"I've been on Earth myself," said Casher, rather drily. "It's not that unusual."

The man stopped with surprise.

"My name," said Casher, "is Casher O'Neill."

The man halted and then gave a deep bow.

"If you are Casher O'Neill, you have changed this world; you have come back, my lord and master. Welcome. We are no longer your host. This is your city. What do you wish of us?"

"To look a while, to rest a while, to ask directions for the voyage."

"Directions? Why should anyone want directions away from here? People come here and ask directions from a thousand places to get to Kermesse Dorgüeil."

"Let's not argue this now," said Casher. "Show us the rooms, let us clean ourselves up. Two separate rooms."

Howard walked upstairs. With an intricate twist of his hand he unlocked two rooms.

"At your service," he said. "Call me with your voice; I can hear you anywhere in the building."

Casher called once for sleeping gear, toothbrushes, shaving equipment. He insisted that they send the shampooer, a woman of apparent Earth origin, in to attend to D'alma; and D'alma actually knocked at his door and begged that he not shower her with these attentions.

He said, "You with your deep kindness have helped me so far. I am helping you very little."

They ate a light repast together in the garden just below their two rooms, and then they went to their rooms and slept.

*   *   *

It was only on the morning of the second day that they went with Howard into the city to see what could be found.

Everywhere the city was strong with happiness. The population could not have been very large, twenty or thirty thousand persons at most.

At one point, Casher stopped; he could smell the scorch of ozone in the air. He knew the atmosphere itself had been burned and that meant only one thing, spaceships coming in or going out.

He asked, "Where is the spaceport for Earth?"

Howard looked at him quickly and keenly. "If you were not the lord Casher O'Neill, I'd never tell you. We have a small spaceport there. That is the way we avoid our traffic with most of Mizzer. Do you need it, sir?"

"Not now," said Casher, "I just wondered where it was." They came to a woman who danced as she sang to the accompaniment of two men with wild archaic guitars. Her feet did not have the laughter of ordinary dance, but they had the positiveness, compulsion of a meaning. Howard looked at her appreciatively; he even ran the tip of his tongue across his upper lip.

"She is not yet spoken for," said Howard. "And yet she is a very unusual thing. A resigned ex-lady of the Instrumentality."

"I find that unusual, indeed. What is her name?"

"Celalta," said Howard. "Celalta, the other one. She has been in many worlds, perhaps as many worlds as you have, sir. She's faced dangers like the ones you've faced. And oh, my lord and master, forgive me for saying it, but when I look at her dancing, and I see you looking at her, I can see a little bit into the future; and I can see you both dead together, the winds slowly blowing the flesh off your bones. And your bones anonymous and white, lying two valleys over from this very place."

"That's an odd enough prophecy," said Casher. "Especially from someone who seems not to be poetic. What is that?"

"I seem to see you in the Deep Dry Lake of the Damned Irene. There's a road out of here that goes there and some people, not many, go there, and when they go there, they die. I don't know why," said Howard, "don't ask me."

D'alma whispered, "That is the road to the Shrine of Shrines. that's the place to the Quel itself. Find out where it starts."

"Where does that road start?" asked Casher.

"Oh, you'll find out; there's nothing you won't find out. Sorry, my lord and master. The road starts just beyond that bright orange roof." He pointed to a roof and then turned back.

Without saying anything more, he clapped his hands at the dancer and she gave him a scornful look. Howard clapped his hands again; she stopped dancing and walked over.

"And what is it you want now, Howard?"

He gave her a deep bow. "My former lady, my mistress, here is the lord and master of this planet, Casher O'Neill."

"I am not really the lord and master," said Casher O'Neill. "I merely would have been if Wedder had not taken the rule away from my uncle."

"Should I care about that?" asked the woman.

Casher smile back. "I don't see why you should."

"Do you have anything you want to say to me?"

"Yes," said Casher. He reached over and seized her wrist. Her wrist was almost as strong as his.

"You have danced your last dance, madam, at least for the time. You and I are going to a place that this man knows about, and he says that we are going to die there, and our bones will be blown with the wind."

"You give me commands," she cried.

"I give you commands," he said.

"What is your authority?" she asked scornfully.

"Me," he said.

She looked at him, he looked back at her, still holding her wrist.

She said, "I have powers. Don't make me use them."

He said, "I have powers, too; nobody can make me use mine."

"I'm not afraid of you, go ahead."

Fire shot at him as he felt the lunge of her mind toward his, her attack, her flight for freedom, but he kept her wrist and she said nothing.

But with his mind responding to hers he unfolded the many worlds, the old Earth itself, the gem planet, Olympia of the blind brooks, the storm planet, Henriada, and a thousand other places that most people only knew in stories and dreams. And then, just for a little bit, he showed her who he was, a native of Mizzer who had become a citizen of the Universe. A fighter who had been transformed into a doer. He let her know that in his own mind he carried the powers of T'ruth the turtle-girl, and behind T'ruth herself, he carried the personalities of the Hechizera of Gonfalon. He let her see the ships in the sky turning and twisting as they fought nothing at all, because his mind, or another mind which had become his, had commanded them to.

And then with the shock of a sudden vision, he projected to her the two pieces of wood, the image of a man in pain. And gently, but with the simple rhetoric of profound faith, he pronounced: "This is the call of the First Forbidden One and the Second Forbidden One and the Third Forbidden One. This is the symbol of the Sign of the Fish. For this you are going to leave this town and you are going with me, and it may be that you and I shall become lovers."

Behind him a voice spoke, "And I," said D'alma, "will stay here."

He turned around to her. "D'alma, you've come this far, you've got to come further."

"I can't, my lord, I read my duty as I see it. If the

authorities who sent me want me enough, they will send me back to my dishwasher on Pontoppidan, otherwise they will leave me here. I am temporarily beautiful and I'm rich and I'm happy and I don't know what to do with myself, but I know I have seen you as far as I can. May the Sign of the Fish be with you."

Howard merely stood aside, making no attempt to hinder them or to help them.

Celalta walked beside Casher like a wild animal which had never been captured before.

Casher O'Neill never let go of her wrist.

"Do we need food for this trip?" he asked of Howard.

"No one knows what you need."

"Should we take food?"

"I don't see why," said Howard. "You have water. You can always walk back here if you have disappointments. It's really not very far."

"Will you rescue me?"

"If you insist on it," said Howard. "I suppose somewhere people will come out and bring you back, but I don't think you will insist—because that is the Deep Dry Lake of the Damned Irene, and the people who go in there do not want to come out, and do not want to eat, and they do not want to go forward. We have never seen anyone vanish to the other side, but you might make it."

"I am looking," said Casher, "for something which is more than power between the worlds. I am looking for a sphinx that is bigger than the sphinx on old Earth. For weapons which cut sharper than lasers, for forces that move faster than bullets. I am looking for something which will take the power away from me and put the simple humanity back into me. I am looking for something which will be nothing, but a nothing I can serve and can believe in."

"You sound like the right kind of man," said Howard, "for that kind of trip. Go in peace, both of you."

Celalta said, "I do not really know who you are, my lord,

master, but I have danced my last dance. I see what you mean. This is the road that leads away from happiness. This is the path which leaves good clothes and warm shops behind. There are not restaurants where we are going, no hotels, no river anymore. There are neither believers nor unbelievers; but there is something that comes out of the soil which makes people die. But if you think, Casher O'Neill, that you can triumph over it, I will go with you. And if you do not think it, I will die with you."

"We are going, Celalta. I didn't know that it was just going to be the two of us, but we are going and we are going now."

X

It was actually less than two kilometers to get over the ridge away from the trees, away from the moisture-laden air along the river and into a dry, calm valley which had a clean blessed quietness which Casher had never seen before.

Celalta was almost gay.

"This, this is the Deep Dry Lake of the Damned Irene?"

"I suppose it is," said Casher, "but I propose to keep on walking. It isn't very big."

As they walked their bodies became burdensome, they carried not only their own weight but the weight of every month of their lives. The decision seemed good to them that they should lie down in the valley and rest amid the skeletons, rest as the others had rested. Celalta became disoriented. She stumbled, and her eyes became unfocused.

Not for nothing had Casher O'Neill learned all the arts of battle of a thousand worlds. Not for nothing had be come through space-three. This valley might have been tempting if he already had not ridden the cosmos on his eyes alone.

He had. He knew the way out. It was merely through. Celalta seemed to come more to life as they reached the top of the ridge. The whole world was suddenly transformed by not less than ten steps. Far behind them, several kilometers, perhaps, there were still visible the last rooftops of the Kermesse Dorgüeil. Behind them lay the bleaching skeletons, in front—

In front of them was the final source and the mystery, the Quel of the Thirteenth Nile.

XI

There was no sign of a house, but there were fruits and melons and grain growing, and there were deep trees at the edges of caves, and there were here and there signs of people that had been there long ago. There were no signs of present occupancy.

"My lord," said the once-lady Celalta, "my lord," she repeated, "I think this is it."

"But this is nothing," said Casher.

"Exactly. Nothing is victory, nothing is arrival, nowhere is getting there. Don't you see now why she left us?"

"She?" asked Casher.

"Yes, your faithful companion, the dog-woman D'alma."

"No, I don't see it. Why did she leave this to us?" Celalta laughed.

"We're Adam and Eve in a way. It's not up to us to be given a god or to be given a faith. It's up to us to find the power and this is the quietest and last of the searching places. The others were just phantoms, hazards on our route. The best way to find freedom is not to look for it, just as you obtained your utter revenge on Wedder by doing him a little bit of good. Can't you see it, Casher? You have won at last the immense victory that makes all battles seem vain. There is food around us; we can even walk back to the Kermesse Dorgüeil, if we want clothing or company or if we want to hear the news. But, most of all, this is the place in which I feel the presence of the First Forbidden One, the Second Forbidden One and the Third Forbidden One. We don't need a church for this, although I suppose there are still churches on some planets. What we need is a place to find ourselves and be ourselves and I'm not sure that this chance exists in many other cases than this one spot."

"You mean," said Casher, "that everywhere is no-where?"

"Not quite that," said Celalta. "We have some work to do getting this place in shape, feeding ourselves. Do you know how to cook? Well, I can cook better. We can catch a few things to eat; we can shut ourselves in that cave and then"—and then Celalta smiled, her face more beautiful than he ever expected he would find a face to be—"we have each other."

Casher stood battle-ready, facing the most beautiful dancer he had ever met. He realized that she had once been a part of the Instrumentality, a governor of worlds, a genuine advisor in the destination of mankind. He did not know what strange motives had caused her to quit authority and to come up to this hard-to-find river, unmarked on maps. He didn't even know why the man Howard should have paired them so quickly: perhaps there was another force. A force behind that dog-woman which had sent him to his final destination.

He looked down at Celalta and then he looked up at the sky, and he said, "Day is ending; I will catch a few of those birds if you know how to cook them. We seem to be a sort of Adam and Eve, and I do not know whether this is paradise or hell. But I know that you are in it with me, and that I can think about you because you ask nothing of me."

"That is true, my lord, I ask nothing of you. I, too, am looking for both of us, not myself alone. I can make a sacrifice for you, but I look for those things which only we two, acting together, can find in this valley."

He nodded in serious agreement.

"Look," she said, "that is the Quel itself, there the Thirteenth Nile comes out of the rocks, and here are the woods below. I seem to have heard of it. Well, we'll have plenty of time. I'll start the fire, but you go catch two of those chickens. I don't even think they're wild birds. I think they are just left over people-chickens that have grown wild since their previous owners left. . . ."

"Or died," said Casher.

"Or died," repeated Celalta. "Isn't that a risk anybody has to take? Let us live, my lord, you and me, and let us find the magic, the deliverance which strange fates have thrown in front of you and me. You have liberated Mizzer, is that not enough? Simply by touching Wedder, you have done what otherwise could have been accomplished at the price of battle and great suffering."

"Thank you," said Casher.

"I was once Instrumentality, my lord, and I know that the Instrumentality likes to do things suddenly and victoriously. When I was there we never accepted defeat, but we never paid anything extra. The shortest route between two points might look like the long way around; it isn't. It's merely the cheapest human way of getting there. Has it ever occurred to you, that the Instrumentality might be rewarding you for what you have done for this planet?"

"I hadn't thought of it," said Casher.

"You hadn't thought of it?" she smiled.

"Well . . ." said Casher, embarrassed and at a loss for words.

"I am a very special kind of woman," said Celalta. "You will be finding that out in the next few weeks. Why else do you think that I would be given to you?"

He did not go to hunt the chickens, not just then. He reached his arms out to her and, with more trust and less fear than he had felt in many years, he held her in his arms, and kissed her on the lips. This time there was no secret reserve in his mind, no promise that after this he would get on with his journey to Mizzer. He had won, his victory was behind him, and in front of him there lay nothing, but this beautiful and powerful place and . . . Celalta.

Part Four

I

"Stick your left arm straight forward, Samm," said Folly.

He stretched his arm out.

"I can sense it!" cried Folly. "Now, wiggle your fingers!"

Samm wiggled them.

Finsternis said nothing, but both of them caught from his mind, riding clear and wise beside them, a "sense of the situation." His "sense of the situation" could be summed up in the one-word comment, which he did not need to utter:

"Foolishness!"

"It is not foolishness, Finsternis," cried Folly. "Here we are the three of us, riding empty space millions of kilometers from nowhere. We were people once, Earth people from Old Earth itself. It is foolish to remember what we used to be? I was a woman once. A beautiful woman. Now I'm this—this thing, bent on a mission of murder and destruction. I used to have hands myself, real hands. Is it wrong for me to enjoy looking at Samm's hands now and then? To think of the past which all three of us have left behind."

Finsternis did not answer; his mind was blank to both of them. There was nothing but space around them, not even much space dust, and the bluish light of Linschoten XV straight ahead. From the third planet of that star they could occasionally hear the cackle and gabble of the man-eaters.

Once again Folly cried to Finsternis, "Is that so wrong, that I should enjoy looking at a hand? Samm has well-shaped hands. I was a person once, and so were you. Did I ever tell you that I was a beautiful woman once?"

She had been a beautiful woman once and now she was the control of a small spaceship which fled across emptiness with two grotesque companions.

She was now a ship only eleven meters long and shaped roughly like an ancient dirigible. Finsternis was a perfect cube, fifty meters to the side, packed with machinery which could blank out a sun and contain its planets until they froze to icy, perpetual death. Samm was a man, but he was a man of flexible steel, two hundred meters high. He was designed to walk on any kind of planet, with any kind of inhabitant, with any kind of chemistry or any kind of gravity. He was designed to bring antagonists, whomever they might be, the message of the power of man. The power of man . . . followed by terror, followed if necessary by death. If Samm failed, Finsternis had the further power of blocking out the sun, Linschoten XV. If either or both failed, Folly had the job of adjusting them so that they could win. If they had no chance of winning, she then had the task of destroying Finsternis and Samm, and then herself.

Their instructions were clear:

"You will not, you will not under any circumstances return. You will not under any conditions turn back toward Earth. You are too dangerous to come anywhere near Earth, ever again. You may live if you wish. If you can. But you must not—repeat *not*—come back. You have your duty. You asked for it. Now you have it. Do not come back. Your forms fit your duty. You will do your duty."

Folly had become a tiny ship, crammed with miniaturized equipment.

Finsternis had become a cube blacker than darkness itself.

Samm had become a man, but a man different from any

which had ever been seen on Earth. He had a metal body, copied from the human form down to the last detail. That way the enemies, whoever they might be, would be given a terrible glimpse of the human shape, the human voice. Two hundred meters high he stood, strong and solid enough to fly through space with nothing but the jets on his belt.

The Instrumentality had designed all three of them. Designed them well.

Designed them to meet the crazy menace out beyond the stars, a menace which gave no clue to its technology or origin, but which responded to the signal "man" with the counter-signal, "gabble cackle! eat, eat! man, man! good to eat! cackle gabble! eat, eat!"

That was enough.

The Instrumentality took steps. And the three of them—the ship, the cube and the metal giant—sped between the stars to conquer, to terrorize, or to destroy the menace which lived on the third planet of Linschoten XV. Or, if needful, to put out that particular sun.

Folly, who had become a ship, was the most volatile of the three.

She had been a beautiful woman once.

II

"You were a beautiful woman once," Samm had said, some years before. "How did you end up becoming a ship?"

"I killed myself," said Folly. "That's why I took this name—Folly. I had a long life ahead of me, but I killed myself and they brought me back at the last minute. When I found out I was still alive, I volunteered for something adventurous, dangerous. They gave me this. Well, I *asked* for it, didn't I?"

"You asked for it," said Samm gravely. Out in the middle of nothing, surrounded by a tremendous lot of nowhere, courtesy was still the lubricant which governed human relations. The two of them observed courtesy and kindness toward one another. Sometimes they threw in a bit of humor, too.

Finsternis did not take part in their talk or their companionship. He did not even verbalize his answers. He merely let them know his sense of the situation and this time, as in all other times, his response was—"Negative. No operation needed. Communication nonfunctional. Not needed here. Silence, please. I kill suns. That is all I do. My part is my business. All mine." This was communicated in a single terrible thought, so that Folly and Samm stopped trying to bring Finsternis into the conversations which they started up, every subjective century or so, and continued for years at a time.

Finsternis merely moved along with them, several kilometers away, but well within their range of awareness. But as far as company was concerned, Finsternis might as well not have been there at all.

Samm went on with the conversation, *the* conversation which they had had so many hundreds of times since the planoform ship had discharged them "near" Linschoten XV and left them to make the rest of their way alone. (If the menace were really a menace, and if it were intelligent, the Instrumentality had no intention of letting an actual planoform ship fall within the powers of a strange form of life which might well be hypnotic in its combat capacities. Hence the ship, the cube and the giant were launched into normal space at high velocity, equipped with jets to correct their courses, and left to make their own way to the danger.)

Samm said, as he always did, "You were a beautiful woman, Folly, but you wanted to die. Why?"

"Why do people ever want to die, Samm? It's the power in us, the vitality which makes us want so much. Life always trembles on the edge of disappointment. If we hadn't been vital and greedy and lustful and yearning, if we hadn't had big thoughts and wanted bigger ones, we would have stayed animals, like all the little things back on Earth. It's strong life that brings us so close to death. We can't stand the beauty of it, the nearness of the things we want, the remoteness of the things that we can have. You and me and Finsternis, now, we're monsters riding out between the stars. And yet we're happier now than we were when we were back among people. I was a beautiful woman, but there were specific things which I wanted. I wanted them myself. I alone. For me. Only for me. When I couldn't have them, I wanted to die. If I had been stupider or happier I might have lived on. But I didn't. I was me—intensely me. So here I am. I don't even know whether I have a body or not, inside this ship. They've got me all hooked up to the sensors and the viewers and the computers. Sometimes I think that I may be a lovely woman still, with a real body hidden somewhere inside this ship, waiting to step out and to be a person again. And you, Samm, don't you want to tell me about yourself? Samm. SAMM. That's no name for an actual person—Superordinated Alien Measuring and Mastery device. What were you before they gave you that big body? At least you still look like a person. You're not a ship, like me."

"My name doesn't matter, Folly, and if I told it to you, you wouldn't know it. You never knew it."

"How wouldn't I know?" she cried. "I've never told you my name either, so perhaps we did know each other back on Old Earth when we were still people."

"I can tell something," said Samm, "from the shape of words, from the ring of thoughts, even when we're not out here in nothing. You were a lady, perhaps highborn. You were truly beautiful. You were really important. And I—I was a technician. A good one. I did my work and I loved my family, and my wife and I were happy with every child which the Lords gave us for adoption. But my wife died first. And after a while my children, my wonderful boy and my two beautiful, intelligent girls—my own children, they couldn't stand me anymore. They didn't like me. Perhaps I talked too much. Perhaps I gave them too much advice. Perhaps I reminded them of their mother, who was dead. I don't know. I won't ever know. They didn't want to see me. Out of manners, they sent me cards on my birthday. Out of sheer formal courtesy, they called on me sometimes. Now and then one of them wanted something. Then they came to me, but it was always just to get something. It took me a long time to figure out, but I hadn't done anything. It wasn't what I had done or hadn't done. They just plain didn't like me. You know the songs and the operas and the stories, Folly, you know them all."

"Not all of them," thought Folly gently, "not all of them. Just a few thousand."

"Did you ever see one," cried Samm, his thoughts ringing fiercely against her mind, "did you ever see a single one about a rejected father? They're all about men and women, love and sex, but I can tell you that rejection hurts even when you don't ask anything of your loved ones but their company and their happiness and their simple genuine smiles. When I knew that my children had no use for me, I had no use for me either. The Instrumentality came along with this warning, and I volunteered."

"But you're all right now, Samm," said Folly gently. "I'm a ship and you are a metal giant, but we're off doing work which is important for all mankind. We'll have adventures together. Even black and grumbly here," she added, meaning Finsternis, "can't keep us from the excitement of companionship or the hope of danger. We're doing something wonderful and important and exciting. Do you know what I would do if I had my life again, my ordinary life with skin and toenails and hair and things like that?"

"What?" asked Samm, knowing the answer perfectly well from the hundreds of times they had touched on this point.

"I'd take baths. Hundreds and hundreds of them, over again. Showers and dips in cold pools and soaks in hot bathtubs and rinses and more showers. And I would do my hair, over and over again, thousands of different ways. And I would put on lipstick, in the most outrageous colors, even if nobody saw me, except for my own self looking in the mirror. Now I can hardly remember what it used to be to be dry or wet. I'm in this ship and I see the ship and I do not really know if I am a person or not any more."

Samm stayed quiet, knowing what she would say next.

"Samm, what would you do?" Folly asked.

"Swim," he said.

"Then swim, Samm, swim! Swim for me in the space between the stars. You still have a body and I don't, but I can watch you and I can sense you swimming out here in the nothing-at-all."

Samm began to swim a huge Australian crawl, dipping his face to the edge of the water—as if there were water there. The gestures made no difference in his real motion, since they were all of them in the fast trajectory computed for them from the point where they left the Instrumentality's ship and started out in normal space for the star listed as Linschoten XV.

This time, something very sudden happened, and, it happened strangely.

From the dark gloomy silence of the cube, Finsternis, there came an articulate cry, called forth in clear human speech:

Stop it! Stop moving right now. I attack.

Both Samm aand Folly had instruments built into them,

so they could read space around them. The instruments, quickly scanned, showed nothing. Yet Folly felt odd, as though something had gone very wrong in her ship-self, which had seemed so metal, so reliable, so inalterable.

She threw a thought of inquiry at Samm and instead got another command from Finsternis. *Don't think.*

III

Samm floated like a dead man in his gargantuan body.

Folly drifted like a fruit beside his hand.

At last there came words from Finsternis:

"You can think now, if you want to. You can chatter at each other again. I'm through."

Samm thought at him, and the thought-pattern was troubled and confused. "What happened? I felt as though the immaculate grid of space had been pinched together in a tight fold. I felt you do something, and then there was silence around us again."

"Talking," said Finsternis, "is not operational and it is not required of me. But there are only three of us here, so I might as well tell you what happened. Can you hear me, Folly?"

"Yes," she said, weakly.

"Are we on course," asked Finsternis, "for the third planet of Linschoten XV?"

Folly paused while checking all her instruments, which were more complicated and refined than those carried by the other two, since she was the maintenance unit. "Yes," said she at last. "We are exactly on course. I don't know what happened, if anything did happen."

"Something happened, all right," said Finsternis, with the gratified savagery of a person whose quick-and-cruel nature is rewarded only by meeting and overcoming hostility in real life.

"Was it a space dragon, like they used to meet on the old, old ships?"

"No, nothing like that," said Finsternis, communicative for once, since this was something operational to talk about. "It doesn't even seem to be in this space at all. Something just rises up among us, like a volcano coming out of solid space. Something violent and wild and alive. Do you two still have eyes?"

"Seeing devices for the ordinary light band?" asked Samm.

"Of course we do!" said Finsternis. "I will try to fix it so that you will have visible input."

There was a sharp pause from Finsternis.

The voice came again, with much strain.

"Do not do anything. Do not try to help me. Just watch. If it wins, destroy me quickly. It might try to capture us and get back on Earth."

Folly felt like telling Finsternis that this was unnecessary, since the first motion toward return would trigger destruction devices which had been built into each of the three of them, beyond reach, beyond detection, beyond awareness. When the Instrumentality said, "Do *not* come back," the Instrumentality meant it.

She said nothing.

She watched Finsternis instead.

Something began to happen. It was very odd.

Space itself seemed to rip and leak.

In the visible band, the intruder looked like a fountain of water being thrown randomly to and fro.

But the intruder was not water.

In the visible light-band, it glowed like wild fire rising from a shimmering column of blue ice. Here in space there was nothing to burn, nothing to make light: she knew that Finsternis was translating unresolvable phenomena into light.

She sensed Samm moving one of his giant fists uncontrollably, in a helpless, childish gesture of protest.

She herself did nothing but watch, as alertly and passively as she could.

Nevertheless, she felt wrenched. This was no material phenomenon. It was wild unformed life, intruding out of some other proportion of space, seeking material on which to impose its vitality, its frenzy, its identity. She could see Finsternis as a solid black cube, darker than mere darkness, drifting right into the column. She watched the sides of Finsternis.

On the earlier part of the trip, since they had left the people and the planoform ship and had been discharged in a fast trajectory toward Linschoten XV, Finsternis' side had seemed like dull metal, slightly burnished, so that Folly had to brush him lightly with radar to get a clear image of him.

Now his sides had changed.

They had become as soft and thick as velvet.

The strange volcano-fountain did not seem to have much in the way of sensing devices. It paid no attention to Samm or to herself. The dark cube attracted it, as a shaft of sunlight might attract a baby or as the rustle of paper might draw the attention of a kitten.

With a slight twist of its vitality and direction, the whole column of burning, living brightness plunged upon Finsternis, plunged and burned out and went in and was seen no more.

Finsternis' voice, clear and cheerful, sounded out to both of them.

"It's gone now."

"What happened to it?" asked Samm.

"I ate it," said Finsternis.

"You what?" cried Folly.

"I ate it," said Finsternis. He was talking more than he ever had before. "At least, that's the only way I can describe it. This machine they gave me or made me into or whatever they did, it's really rather good. It's powerful. I can feel it absorbing things, taking them in, taking them apart, putting them away. It's something like eating used to be when I was a person. That wild thing attacked me, wrapped me up, devoured me. All I did was to take it in, and now it's gone. I feel sort of full. I suppose my machines are sorting out samples of it to send away to rendezvous points in little rockets. I know that I have sixteen small rockets inside me, and I can feel two of them getting ready to move. Neither one of you could have done what I do. I was built to absorb whole suns if necessary, break them down, freeze them down, change their molecular structure and shoot their vitality off in one big useless blast on the radio spectrum. You couldn't do anything like that, Samm, even if you do have arms and legs and a head and a voice— if we ever get into an atmosphere for you to use it in. You couldn't do what I have just done, Folly."

"You're *good*," said Folly, with emphasis. But she added: "I can repair *you*."

Obviously offended, Finsternis withdrew into his silence. Samm said to Folly, "How much further to destination?"

Said Folly promptly, "Seventy-nine earth years, four months and three days, six hours and two minutes, but you know how little that means out here. It could seem like a single afternoon or it could feel to us like a thousand lifetimes. Time doesn't work very well for us."

"How did Earth ever find this place, anyhow?" asked Samm.

"All I know is that it was two very strong telepaths, working together on the planet Mizzer. An ex-dictator named Casher O'Neill and an ex-Lady named Celalta. They were doing a bit of psionic astronomy and suddenly this signal came in strong and clear. You know that telepaths can catch directions very accurately. Even over immense distances. And they can get emotions, too. But they are not very good at actual images or things. Somebody else checked it out for them."

"M-m-m," said Samm. He had heard all this before. Out of sheer boredom, he went back to swimming vigorously. The body might not really be his, but it made him feel good to exercise it.

Besides, he knew that Folly watched him with pleasure— great pleasure, and a little bit of envy.

Casher O'Neill and the Lady Celalta had finished with making love.

They had lain with their bodies tired and their minds clear, relaxed. They had stretched out on a blanket just above the big gushing spring which was the source of the Ninth Nile. Both telepaths, they could hear a bird-couple quarreling inside a tree, the male bird commanding the female to get out and get to work and the female answering by dropping deeper and deeper into a fretful and irritable sleep.

The Lady Celalta had whispered a thought to her lover and master, Casher O'Neill.

"To the stars?"

"The stars?" thought he with a grumble. They were both strong telepaths. He had been imprinted, in some mysterious way, with the greatest telepath-hypnotist of all time, the Honorable Agatha Madigan. In the Lady Celalta he had a companion worthy of his final talents, a natural telepath who could herself reach not only all of Mizzer but some of the nearer stars. When they teamed up together, as she now proposed, they could plunge into dusty infinites of depth and bring back feelings or images which no Go-Captain had ever found with his ship.

He sat up with a grunt of assent.

She looked at him fondly, possessively, her dark eyes alight with alertness, happiness, and adventure.

"Can I lift?" she asked, almost timidly.

When two telepaths worked together, one cleared the vision for both of them as far as their combined minds could reach and then, the other sprang, with enormous effort as far and as fast as possible toward any target which presented itself. They had found strange things, sometimes beautiful or dramatic ones, by this method.

Casher was already drinking enormous gulps of air, filling his lungs, holding his breath, letting go with a gasp and then inhaling deeply and slowly again. In this way he reoxygenated his brain very thoroughly for the huge effort of a telepathic dive into the remote depth of space. He did not even speak to her, nor did he telepath a word to her; he was conserving his strength for a good jump.

He merely nodded to her.

The Lady Celalta, too, began the deep breathing, but she seemed to need it less than did Casher.

They were both sitting up, side by side, breathing deeply.

The cool night sands of Mizzer were around them, the harmless gurgle of the Ninth Nile beside them, the bright star-cluttered sky of Mizzer was above them.

Her hand reached out and took hold of his. She squeezed his hand. He looked at her and nodded to her again.

Within his mind, Mizzer and its entire solar system seemed to burst into flame and with a new kind of light. The radiance of Celalta's mind trailed off unevenly in different directions, but there, almost 2° off the pole of Mizzer's ecliptic, he felt something wild and strange, a kind of being which he had never sensed before. Using Celalta's mind as a base, he let his mind dive for it.

The distance of the plunge left them both dizzy, sitting on the quiet night sands of Mizzer. It seemed to both of them that the mind of man had never reached so far before.

The reality of the phenomenon was undoubtable.

There were animals all around them, the usual categories: runners, hunters, jumpers, climbers, swimmers, hiders and handlers. It was some of the handlers who were intensely telepathic themselves.

The image of man created an immediate, murderous response.

"Cackle gabble, gabble cackle, man, man, man, eat them, eat them!"

Casher and Celalta were both so surprised that they let the contact go, after making sure that they had touched a whole world full of beings, some of them telepathic and probably civilized.

How had the beings known "man"? Why had their response been immediate? Why anthropophagous and homicidal?

They took time, before coming completely out of the trance, to make a careful, exact note of the direction from which the danger-brains had shrieked their warning.

This they submitted to the Instrumentality, shortly after the incident.

And that was how, unknown to Folly, Samm and Finsternis, the inhabitants on the third planet of Linschoten XV had come to the attention of mankind.

IV

As a matter of fact, the three wanderers later on felt a vague, remote telepathic contact which they sensed as being warmhearted and human, and therefore did not try to track down, with their minds or their weapons. It was O'Neill and Celalta, many years later, by Mizzer time, reaching to see what the Instrumentality had done about Linschoten XV.

Folly, Samm and Finsternis had no suspicion that the two most powerful telepaths in the human area of the galaxy had stroked them, searched them, felt them through, and seen things about them which the three of them did not know about themselves or about each other.

Casher O'Neill said to the Lady Celalta, "You got it, too?"

"A beautiful woman, encased in a little ship?"

Casher nodded. "A redhead with skin as soft and transparent as living ivory? A woman who was beautiful and will be beautiful again?"

"That's what I got," said the Lady Celalta. "And the tired old man, weary of his children and weary of his own life because his children were weary of him."

"Not so old," said Casher O'Neill. "And isn't that a spectacular piece of machinery they put him into? A metal giant. It felt like something about a quarter of a kilometer high. Acid-proof. Cold-proof. Won't he be surprised when he finds that the Instrumentality has rejuvenated his own body inside that monster?"

"He certainly will be," said the Lady Celalta happily, thinking of the pleasant surprise which lay ahead of a man whom she would never know or see with her own bodily eyes.

They both fell silent.

Then said the Lady Celalta, "But the third person . . ." There was a shiver in her voice as though she dared not ask the question. "The third person, the one in the cube." She stopped, as though she could neither ask nor say more.

"It was not a robot or a personality cube," said Casher O'Neill. "It was a human being all right. But it's crazy. Could you make out, Celalta, as to whether it was male or female?"

"No," said she, "I couldn't tell. The other two seemed to think that it was male."

"But did *you* feel sure?" asked Casher.

"With that being, I felt sure of nothing. It was human, all right, but it was stranger than any lost hominid we have ever felt around the forgotten stars. Could you tell, Casher, whether it was young or old?"

"No," said he. "I felt nothing—only a desperate human mind with all its guards up, living only because of the terrible powers of the black cube, the sun-killer in which it rode. I never sensed someone before who was a person without characteristics. It's frightening."

"The Instrumentality are cruel sometimes," said Celalta.

"Sometimes they have to be," Casher agreed.

"But I never thought that they would do that."

"Do what?" asked Casher.

Her dark eyes looked at him. It was a different night, and a different Nile, but the eyes were only a very little bit older and they loved him just as much as ever. The Lady Celalta trembled as though she herself might think that the all-powerful Instrumentality could have hidden a microphone in the random sands. She whispered to her lover, "You said it yourself, Casher, just a moment ago."

"Said what?" He spoke tenderly but fearlessly, his voice ringing out over the cool night sands.

The Lady Celalta went on whispering, which was very unlike her usual self. "You said that the third person was 'crazy.' Do you realize that you may have spoken the actual literal truth?" Her whisper darted at him like a snake.

At last, he whispered back, "What did you sense? What could you guess?"

"They have sent a madman to the stars. Or a mad woman. A real psychotic."

"Lots of pilots," said Casher, speaking more normally, "are cushioned against loneliness with real but artificially activated psychoses. It gets them through the real or imagined horrors of the sufferings of space."

"I don't mean that," said Celalta, still whispering urgently and secretly. "I mean a real psychotic."

"But there aren't any. Not loose, that is," said Casher, stammering with surprise at last. "They either get cured or they are bottled up in thought-proof satellites somewhere."

Celalta raised her voice a little, just a little, so that she no longer whispered but spoke urgently.

"But don't you see, that's what they *must* have done. The Instrumentality made a star-killer too strong for any normal mind to guide. So the Lords got a psychotic somewhere, a real psychotic, and sent a madman out among the stars. Otherwise we could have felt its gender or its age."

Casher nodded in silent agreement. The air did not feel colder, but he got gooseflesh sitting beside his beloved Celalta on the familiar desert sands.

"You're right. You must be right. It almost makes me feel sorry for the enemies out near Linschoten XV. Do you see nothing of them this time? I couldn't perceive them at all."

"I did, a little," said the Lady Celalta. "Their telepaths have caught the strange minds coming at them with a high rate of speed. The telepathic ones are wild with excitement but the others are just going cackle-gabble, cackle-gabble with each other, filled with anger, hunger and the thought of man."

"You got that much?" he said in wonder.

"My lord and my lover, I dived this time. Is it so strange that I sensed more than you did? Your strength lifted me."

"Did you hear what the weapons called each other?"

"Something silly." He could see her knitting her brows in the bright starshine which illuminated the desert almost the way that the Old Original Moon lit up the nights sometimes on Manhome itself. "It was Folly, and something like 'Superordinated Alien Measuring and Mastery machine' and something like 'darkness' in the Ancient Doyches Language."

"That's what I got, too," said Casher. "It sounds like a weird team."

"But a powerful one, a terribly powerful one," said the Lady Celalta. "You and I, my lover and master, have seen strange things and dangers between the stars, even before we met each other, but we never saw anything like this before, did we?"

"No," said he.

"Well, then," said she, "let us sleep and forget the matter as much as we can. The Instrumentality is certainly taking care of Linschoten XV, and we two need not bother about it."

And all that Samm, Folly and Finsternis knew was that a light touch, unexplained but friendly, had gone over them from the far star region near home. Thought they, if they thought anything about it at all, "The Instrumentality, which made us and sent us, has checked up on us one more time."

V

A few years later, Samm and Folly were talking again while Finsternis—guarded, impenetrable, uncommunicating, detectable only by the fierce glow of human life which shone telepathically out of the immense cube—rode space beside them and said nothing.

Suddenly Folly cried out to Samm loudly. "I can *smell* them."

"Smell who?" asked Samm mildly. "There isn't any smell out here in the nothingness of space."

"Silly," thought Folly back, "I don't mean really smell. I mean that I can pick up *their* sense of odor telepathically."

"Whose?" said Samm, being dense.

"Our enemies', of course," cried Folly. "The man-rememberers who are not man. The cackle-gabble creatures. The beings who remember man and hate him. They smell thick and warm and alive to each other. Their whole world is full of smells. Their telepaths are getting frantic now. They have even figured out that there are three of us and they are trying to get our smells."

"And we have no smell. Not when we do not even know whether we have human bodies or not, inside these things. Imagine this metal body of mine smelling. If it did have a smell," said Samm, "it would probably be the very soft smell of working steel and a little bit of lubricants, plus whatever odors my jets might activate inside an atmosphere. If I know the Instrumentality, they have made my jets smell awful to almost any kind of being. Most forms of life think first through their noses and then figure out the rest of experience later. After all, I was built to intimidate, to frighten, to destroy. The Instrumentality did not make this giant to be friendly with anybody. You and I can be friends, Folly, because you are a little ship which I could hold like a cigar between my fingers, and because the ship holds the memory of a very lovely woman. I can sense what you once were. What you may still be, if your actual body is still inside that boat."

"Oh, Samm!" she cried. "Do you think I might still be alive, really alive, with a real me in a real me, and a chance to be myself somewhere again, out here between the stars?"

"I can't sense it plainly," said Samm. "I've reached as much as I can through your ship with my sensors, but I can't tell whether there's a whole woman there or not. It might be just a memory of you dissected and laminated between a lot of plastic sheets. I really can't tell, but sometimes I have the strangest hunch that you are still alive, in the old ordinary way, and that I am alive too."

"Wouldn't that be wonderful!" She almost shouted at him. "Samm, imagine being us again, if we fulfill our mission and conquer this planet and stay alive and settle there! I might even meet you and—"

They both fell silent at the implications of being ordinary-alive again. They knew that they loved each other. Out here, in the immense blackness of space, there was nothing they could do but streak along in their fast trajectories and talk to each other a little bit by telepathy.

"Samm," said Folly, and the tone of her thought showed that she was changing a difficult subject. "Do you think that we are the furthest out that people have ever gone? You used to be a technician. You might know. Do you?"

"Of course I know," thought Samm promptly. "We're not. After all, we're still deep inside our own galaxy."

"I didn't know," said Folly contritely.

"With all those instruments, don't you know where you are?"

"Of course I know where I am, Samm. In relation to the third planet of Linschoten XV. I even have a faint idea of the general direction in which Old Earth must lie, and how many thousands of ages it would take us to get home, traveling through ordinary space, if we did try to turn around." She thought to herself but didn't add in her thought to Samm, "Which we can't." She thought again to him, "But I've never studied astronomy or navigation, so I couldn't tell whether we were at the edge of the galaxy or not."

"Nowhere near the edge," said Samm. "We're not John Joy Tree and we're nowhere near the two-headed elephants which weep forever in intergalactic space."

"John Joy Tree?" sang Folly; there was joy and memory in her thoughts as she sounded the name. "He was my idol when I was a girl. My father was a subchief of the Instrumentality and always promised to bring John Joy Tree to our house. We had a country and it was unusual and very fine for this day and age. But mister and Go-Captain Tree never got around to visiting us, so there I was, a big girl with picture-cubes of him all over my room. I liked him because he was so much older than me, and so resolute-looking and so tender too. I had all sorts of romantic day-dreams about him, but he never showed up and I married the wrong man several times, and my children got given to the wrong people, so here I am. But what's this stuff about two-headed elephants?"

"Really?" said Samm. "I don't see how you could hear about John Joy Tree and not know what he did."

"I knew he flew far, far out, but I didn't know exactly what he did. After all, I was just a child when I fell in love with his picture. What *did* he do? He's dead now, I suppose, so I don't suppose it matters."

Finsternis cut in, grimly and unexpectedly, "John Joy Tree is not dead. He's creeping around a monstrous place on an abandoned planet, and he is immortal and insane."

"How did you know that?" cried Samm, turning his enormous metal head to look at the dark burnished cube which had said nothing for so many years.

There was no further thought from Finsternis, not a ghost, not an echo of a word.

Folly prodded him. "It's no use trying to make that thing talk if it doesn't want to. We've both tried, thousands of times. Tell me about the two-headed elephants. Those are the big animals with large floppy ears and the noses that pick things up, aren't they? And they make very wise, dependable underpeople out of them?"

"I don't know about the underpeople part, but the animals are the kind you mention, very big indeed. When John Joy Tree got far outside our cosmos by flying through space he found an enormous procession of open ships flying in columns where there was nothing at all. The ships were made by nothing which man has ever even seen. We still don't know where they came from or what made them. Each open ship had a sort of animal, something like an elephant with four front legs and a head at each end, and as he passed the unimaginable ships, these animals howled at him. Howled grief and mourning. Our best guess was that the ships were the tombs of some great race of beings and the howling elephants, the immortal half-living mourners who guarded them."

"But how did John Joy Tree ever get back?"

"Ah, that was beautiful. If you go into space-three, you take nothing more than your own body with you. That was the finest engineering the human race has ever done. They designed and built a whole planoform ship out of John Joy Tree's skin, fingernails and hair. They had to change his body chemistry a bit to get enough metal in him to carry the coils and the electric circuits, but it worked. He came back.

That was a man who could skip through space like a little
boy hopping on familiar rocks. He's the only pilot who ever
piloted himself back home from outside our galaxy. I don't
know whether it will be worth the time and treasure to use
space-three for intergalactic trips. After all, some very
gifted people may have already fallen through by accident,
Folly. You and Finsternis and I are people who have been
built into machines. We are now ourselves the machines.
But with Tree they did it the other way around. They made a
machine out of *him*. And it worked. In that one deep flight
he went billions of times further than we will ever go."

"You think you know," said Finsternis unexpectedly.
"That's what you always do. You think you know."

Folly and Samm tried to get Finsternis to talk some more,
but nothing happened. After a few more rests and talks they
were ready for landing on the third planet of Linschoten XV.

They landed.

They fought.

Blood ran on the ground. Fire scorched the valleys and
boiled the lakes. The telepathic world was full of the cackle-
gabble of fright, hatred throwing itself into suicide, fury
turning into surrender, into deep despair, into hopelessness,
and at last into a strange kind of quiet and love.

Let us not tell that story.

It can be written some other time, told by some other
voice.

The beings died by thousands and tens of thousands while
Finsternis sat on a mountain-top, doing nothing. Folly wove
death and destruction, uncoded languages, drew maps,
showed Samm the strong-points and the weapons which had
to be destroyed. Part of the technology was very advanced,
other parts were still tribal. The dominant race was that of
the beings who had evolved into handlers and thinkers; it
was they who were the telepaths.

All hatred ceased as the haters died. Only the submissive
ones lived on.

Samm tore cities about with his bare metal hands, ripped heavy guns to pieces while they were firing at him, picking the gunners off the gun carriages as though they were lice, swimming oceans when he had to, with Folly darting and hovering around or ahead of him.

Final surrender was brought by their strongest telepath, a very wise old male who had been hidden inside a deep mountain.

"You have come, people. We surrender. Some of us have always known the truth. We are Earth-born, too. A cargo of chickens settled here unimaginable times ago. A time-twist tore us out of our convoy and threw us here. That's why, when we sensed you far across space, we caught the relationship of eat-and-eaten. Only, our brave ones had it wrong. You eat us: we don't eat you. You are the masters now. We will serve you forever. Do you seek our death?"

"No, no," said Folly. "We came only to avert a danger, and we have done that. Live on, and on, but plan no war and make no weapons. Leave that to the Instrumentality."

"Blessed is the Instrumentality, whoever that may be. We accept your terms. We belong to you."

When this was done, the war was over.

Strange things began to happen.

Wild voices sang from within Folly and Samm, voices not their own. *Mission gone. Work finished. Go to hill with cube. Go and rejoice!*

Samm and Folly hesitated. They had left Finsternis where they landed, halfway around the planet.

The singing voices became more urgent. *Go. Go. Go now. Go back to the cube. Tell the chicken-people to plant a lawn and a grove of trees. Go, go, go now to the good reward!*

They told the telepaths what had been said to them and voyaged wearily up out of the atmosphere and back down for a landing at the original point of contact, a long low hill which had been planted with huge patches of green turf and freshly transplanted trees even in the hours in which they flew off the world and back on it again. The bird-telepaths must have had strong and quick commands.

The singing became pure music as they landed, chorales of reward and rejoicing, with the hint of martial marches and victory fugues woven in.

Alan, stand up, said the voices to Samm.

Samm stood on the ridge of the hill. He stood like a colossus against the red-dawning sky. A friendly, quiet crowd of the chicken-people fell back.

Alan, put your hand to your right forehead, sang the voices.

Samm obeyed. He did not know why the voices called him "Alan."

Ellen, land, sang the rejoicing voices to Folly. Folly, herself a little ship, landed at Samm's feet. She was bewildered with happy confusion and a great deal of pain which did not seem to matter much.

Alan, come forth, sang the voices. Samm felt a sharp pain as his forehead—his huge metal forehead, two hundred meters above the ground—burst open and closed again. There was something pink and helpless in his hand.

The voices commanded, *Alan, put your hand gently on the ground.*

Samm obeyed and put his hand on the ground. The little pink toy fell on the fresh truf. It was a tiny miniature of a man.

Ellen, stand forth, sang the voices again. The ship named Folly opened a door and a naked young woman fell out.

Alma, wake up. The cube named Finsternis turned darker than charcoal. Out of the dark side, there stumbled a black-haired girl. She ran across the hill-slope to the figure named Ellen. The man-body named Alan was struggling to his feet.

The three of them stood up.

The voices spoke to them: *This is our last message. You have done your work. You are well. The boat named Folly contains tools, medicine and the other equipment for a human colony. The giant named Samm will stand forever as a monument to human victory. The cube named Finsternis will now dissolve. Alan! Ellen! Treat Alma lovingly and well. She is now a forgetty.*

The three naked people stood bewildered in the dawn.

"Good-bye and a great high thanks from the Instrumentality. This is a pre-coded message, effective only if you won. You have won. Be happy. Live on!"

Ellen took Alma—who had been Finsternis—and held her tight. The great cube dissolved into a shapeless slag-heap. Alan, who had been Samm, looked up at his former body dominating the skyline.

For reasons which the travelers did not understand until many years had passed, the bird-people around them broke into ululant hymns of peace, welcome and joy.

"My house," said Ellen, pointing at the little ship which had spat forth her body just minutes ago, "is now a home for all of us."

They climbed into the successful little ship which had been called Folly. They knew, somehow, that they would find clothes and food. And wisdom, too. They did.

VI

Ten years later, they had the proof of happiness playing in the yard before their house—a substantial building, made of stone and brick, which the local people had built under Alan's directions. (They had changed their whole technology in the process of learning from him, and—thanks to the efficiency and power of the telepathic priestly caste—things learned at any one spot on the planet were swiftly disseminated to the whole group of races on the planet.) The proof of happiness consisted of the thirty-five human children playing in the yard. Ellen had had nine, four sets of twins and a single. Alma had had twelve, two sets of quintuplets and a pair of twins. The other fourteen had been bottle-grown from ova and sperm which they found in the ship, the frozen donations of complete strangers who had done their bit for the offworld settling of the human race. Thanks to the careful genetic coding of both the womb-children and the bottle-children, there was a variety of types, suitable for natural breeding over many generations to come.

Alan came to the door. He measured the time by the place where the great shadow fell. It was hard to realize that the gigantic, indestructible statue which loomed above them all had once been his own self. A small glacier was beginning to form around the feet of Samm and the night was getting cold.

"I'm bringing the children in already," said Ch-tikkik,

one of the local nurses they had hired to help with the huge brood of human babies. She, in return, got the privilege of hatching her eggs on the warm shelf behind the electric stove; she turned them every hour, eagerly awaiting the time that sharp little mouths would break the shell and humanlike little hands would tear an opening from which a humanlike baby would emerge, oddly-pretty-ugly like a gnome, and unusual only in that it could stand upright from the moment of birth.

One little boy was arguing with Ch-tikkik. He wore a warm robe of vegetable-fiber veins knitted to serve as a base for a feather cloak. He was pointing out that with such a robe he could survive a blizzard and claiming, quite justly, that he did not have to be in the house in order to stay warm. *Was that Rupert?* thought Alan.

He was about to call the child when his two wives came to the door, arm in arm, flushed with the heat of the kitchen where they had been cooking the two dinners together—one dinner for the humans, now numbering thirty-eight, and the other for the bird-people, who were tremendously appreciative of getting cooked food, but who had odd requirements in the recipes, such as "one quart of finely ground granite gravel to each gallon of oatmeal, sugared to taste and served with soybean milk."

Alan stood behind his wives and put a hand on the shoulder of each.

"It's hard to think," he said, "that a little over ten years ago, we didn't even know that we were still people. Now look at us, a family, and a good one."

Alma turned her face up to be kissed, and Ellen, who was less sentimental, lifted her face to be kissed, too, so that her co-wife would not be embarrassed at being babied separately. The two liked each other very much. Alma came out of the cube Finsternis as a forgetty, conditioned to remember nothing of her long sad psychotic life before the Instrumentality had sent her on a wild mission among the stars. When she had joined Alan and Ellen, she knew the words of the Old Common Tongue, but very little else.

Ellen had had some time to teach her, to love her and to mother her before any of the babies were born, and the relationship between the two of them was warm and good.

The three parents stood aside as the bird-women, wearing their comfortable and pretty feather cloaks, herded the children into the house. The smallest children had already been brought in from their sunning and were being given their bottles by bird-girls who never got tired of watching the cuteness and helplessness of the human infant.

"It's hard to think of that time at all," said Ellen, who had been "Folly." "I wanted beauty and fame and a perfect marriage and nobody even told me that they just didn't go together. I have had to come to the end of the stars to get what I wanted, to be what I might become."

"And me," said Alma, who had been "Finsternis," "I had a worse problem. I was crazy. I was afraid of life. I didn't even know how to be a woman, a sweetheart, a female, a mother. How could I ever guess that I needed a sister and wife, like the one you have been, to make my life whole? Without you to show me, Ellen, I could never have married our husband. I thought I was carrying murder among the stars, but I was carrying my own solution as well. Where else could I turn out to be me?"

"And I," said Alan, who had been "Samm," "became a metal giant between the stars because my first wife was dead and my own children forgot me and neglected me. Nobody can say I'm not a father now. Thirty-five and more than half of them mine. I'll be more of a father than any other man of the human race has ever been."

There was a change in the shadow as the enormous right arm swung heavily toward the sky as a prelude to the sharp robotic call that nightfall, calculated with astronomical precision, had indeed come to the place where he stood.

The arm reached its height, pointing straight up.

"*I* used to do that," said Alan.

The cry came, something like a silent pistol-shot which all of them heard, but a shot without echoes, without reverberations.

Alan looked around. "All the children are in. Even Rupert. Come in, my darlings, and let us have dinner together." Alma and Ellen went ahead of him and he barred the heavy doors behind them.

This was peace and happiness; that at last was goodness. They had no obligation but to live and to be happy. The threat and the promise of victory were far, far behind.

ABOUT THE AUTHOR

Cordwainer Smith was the pseudonym of Dr. Paul Myron Anthony Linebarger (1913–1966).

A member of the Foreign Policy Association and professor of Asiatic Politics at Johns Hopkins University, Dr. Linebarger was one of America's most competent specialists on the Far East and on psychological warfare.

The son of a retired judge who helped finance the Chinese revolution of 1911, he grew up in China, Japan, France and Germany, learning six languages by his late teens. Sun Yat-sen himself was Linebarger's godfather.

Already involved in diplomatic negotiations at the age of seventeen, Linebarger spent the 1930s assisting his father as legal advisor to Chiang Kai-shek and writing his own authoritative texts on Chinese affairs.

Despite having been blinded in one eye as a child, Linebarger contrived to have himself commissioned in the U.S. Army as an intelligence operative in China during World War II. First named to the office of War Planning, he drew up such stringent specifications for the job that only he could qualify!

As Lt. Col. Linebarger, he again saw service in the Korean War. One of his coups was to persuade Chinese soldiers to give themselves up while saving face by shouting Chinese words which meant things like "honor" and "duty," but which sounded, when spoken in the right order, like "I surrender," in English.

His Korean experience led to his writing *Psychological Warfare*, still regarded as *the* textbook in the field. But he passed up Vietnam, feeling our involvement there was a mistake.

"Scanners Live in Vain," his first science-fiction story as Cordwainer Smith, appeared in 1950. But "War No. 81-Q" had been published in 1928 under the same Anthony Bearden by-line used for poetry quoted in *Norstrilia*; unfortunately, no one can remember where it appeared.

That story, and others that began appearing in 1955, formed parts of a strange history of the future that was a mixture of Oriental and Occidental influence and literary techniques and of scientific and religious philosophy. A High-Church Episcopalian, Linebarger seems to have been striving—perhaps by coincidence—for a synthesis similar to that of Teilhard de Chardin. Smith's shorter stories (a number of which appear in *The Best of Cordwainer Smith* also published by Ballantine Books) trace humanity's rise from the destruction of the Ancient Wars through the adventurous age of space sailors to the decadence of a perfect utopia—all under the ruthless benevolence of the Instrumentality of Mankind.

Norstrilia, Smith's only sf novel, was intended to be the centerpiece of a mosaic of shorter works about the Rediscovery of Man and the Holy Insurgency. These shorter works shed more light on events casually referred to in the novel—previous activities of C'mell and Lord Jestocost, the martyrdom of D'joan and others.

First written in 1960, *Norstrilia* was split into two parts—with material grafted on to make them look like separate novels—for paperback publication elsewhere, following the magazine appearance of excerpts in 1964. This edition is the first appearance anywhere of *Norstrilia* in its original form—something for which all admirers of Smith's work should be grateful.

—J. J. Pierce
June 1978

There's an epidemic with 27 million victims. And no visible symptoms.

It's an epidemic of people who can't read.

Believe it or not, 27 million Americans are functionally illiterate, about one adult in five.

The solution to this problem is you... when you join the fight against illiteracy. So call the Coalition for Literacy at toll-free **1-800-228-8813** and volunteer.

**Volunteer
Against Illiteracy.
The only degree you need
is a degree of caring.**

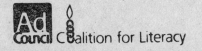

Ad Council Coalition for Literacy

LV-1